The Tower at Moonville

OTHER BOOKS BY STEPHEN ELBOZ

The House of Rats
The Games-Board Map
Bottle Boy
A Store of Secrets
Ghostlands
Temmi and the Flying Bears
A Handful of Magic

The Tower at Moonville

'Look here, Nat,' he began slowly. 'Why not take my place? There—I have made up a plan of escape for both of us.'

'No! It's impossible!' cried Nathan. 'It would never work.'

But it does, at least for a while. Nathan and Sam change places. Sam goes off into the world, to seek adventure, and Nathan finds adventure of a very different kind in the strangest of all schools, Moonville. There are no teachers, no lessons, and the boys are left to run riot. Nathan meets the old scientist who lives in the tower, and he begins to learn all about the stars, the planets, and the possibility of life beyond our universe. But then Nathan's wicked uncle finally tracks him down, and life gets very dangerous indeed.

STEPHEN ELBOZ lives in Northamptonshire, and has had a variety of jobs, including being a dustman, a civil servant, and a volunteer on an archaeological dig. He now divides his time between teaching and writing. His first book, *The House of Rats*, won the Smarties Young Judges Prize for the 9–11 age category.

'Stephen Elboz is an exciting new literary talent.'
The Independent

THE TOWER AT MOONVILLE

Stephen Elboz

OXFORD
UNIVERSITY PRESS

OXFORD
UNIVERSITY PRESS

Great Clarendon Street, Oxford OX2 6DP

Oxford University Press is a department of the University of Oxford.
It furthers the University's objective of excellence in research, scholarship,
and education by publishing worldwide in

Oxford New York

Athens Auckland Bangkok Bogotá Buenos Aires Calcutta
Cape Town Chennai Dar es Salaam Delhi Florence Hong Kong Istanbul
Karachi Kuala Lumpur Madrid Melbourne Mexico City Mumbai
Nairobi Paris São Paulo Singapore Taipei Tokyo Toronto Warsaw

and associated companies in Berlin Ibadan

Oxford is a registered trade mark of Oxford University Press
in the UK and in certain other countries

British Library Cataloguing in Publication Data available

ISBN 0 19 275093 3

Typeset by AFS Image Setters Ltd, Glasgow

Printed in Great Britain

This book is for Clive Dacombe

With special thanks to Liz Evans who typed the manuscript and helped to prepare it for publication

ONE

Nathan Wheatear hated his Uncle Jago and could not remember a time he didn't. When very young he had cried out in terror at the very sight of Jago Blint swaggering down the road with his terrier, Nip, faithfully in step beside him.

In those days it had been Jago's hat which distressed Nathan most. A dusty, shapeless stovepipe worn at a brash angle—similar to a thousand others, except in one respect: Jago was in the habit of hanging three or four freshly killed mice from the brim of his. Strung up by their tails, the mice swayed together in a kind of miniature gallows dance which so bewitched Nathan that he was unable to take his eyes off them.

Peering out from behind his mother's billowing skirts, Nathan would hear the angry edge to her voice. 'Why must you keep on tormenting the poor child so, Jago?' she'd say. 'No wonder he has nightmares, with you looking such a fright in that dreadful old hat.'

Jago, as if wounded by her words, would reply, 'This hat of mine tells the world who I am and what I does. 'Tis nothing to act ashamed of.' Then, with an evil leer towards Nathan, he'd remove the hat from his greasy head and play the strings like the strings on a harp, causing the dead mice to jump and flail and Nathan to scream in terror, 'Tell him to stop, mother!'

Jago's trade was vermin catcher (it accounted for the distinctive smell about him too). The trade had been inherited from his father, who in turn had inherited it from *his* father, and so on and so forth throughout the Blints of history, until it was well known that no one could trap, snare, or poison better than the Blints. And

1

by their work they had come to the notice of no less a person than King Charles II, who had granted the family a licence to rid his streets of its troublesome vermin. Nathan was first shown the scrolled-up document on the very same day he was packed off to live with his Uncle Jago. He was too miserable to be impressed. The ink was so old it was faded and the king's wax seal at the bottom had turned into a shapeless blob. But to make its message clear to those who could not—or would not—read, there were on certain of the capital letters fierce cats pursuing mice nearly as large as themselves, or little stocky dogs tossing rats high up into the air, the way Nip did when he was set to ratting.

The licence was Jago's most prized possession and yet Nathan would have liked nothing better than to have taken a match to its grubby edge and watch it slowly burn. He would burn it for the miserable life he suffered with his uncle. It had begun just a year ago, following the last bad outbreak of typhoid, when three times Nathan had been forced to walk in solemn procession to the graveyard: once for his father, then for his mother, and lastly for Sarah, his baby sister. Jago had worn his disgusting hat at each funeral, removing it only at the church door, each of the hung mice tied with a black bow.

'Never you fear, Nattie,' Jago had whispered excitedly to Nathan, standing beside the graves of his family. 'I'll make a true Blint of you yet. You shall wear a mouse from your cap to show all the world that you're my new apprentice.'

'Never!' cried Nathan and with such passion that other mourners lifted their heads and stared at him.

Jago smiled knowingly. 'Don't think I don't understand, Nattie, but you'll find y'self less squeamish than you thought. 'Tis in your blood, boy, like it's in mine and Nip's.'

Nathan looked down at the freshly turned earth. 'And now do I have to go and live with you, Uncle?' he asked.

'Of course, Nattie, where else is there for you to go?'

Nathan didn't know, but he wished it were some other place, even if it were halfway round the world.

The Blints (for Jago was married to a tall, disagreeable woman named Maudie) lived on the canals in a narrow boat. Not one of those merrily painted ones Nathan had seen carrying cargoes and families and bedecked with washing like the flags of all nations. Jago's boat was coated from bow to stern in thick, sticky pitch and was called *The Lost Hope*. It was a low, dark, sinister vessel, which every few days slid to a different mooring in the half-silted-up backwaters, losing itself among sooty factories and decaying warehouses, moving stealthily through the stinking rust-coloured water and leaking, half-rotted locks, like a malicious crocodile stalking its prey. This constant moving about made Jago feel more secure: some of his business sidelines were not exactly within the law, and it suited him to have a travelling address where the curious could not easily spy on him.

On board, Nathan had the smallest of cabins at the bow. Really it was barely more than an awkwardly shaped cupboard, with just enough room for a narrow bunk and a tiny stove (for heating in winter), but at least it put the length of the boat between him and the terrible Blints, who lived in the main living space at the stern and who were constantly at each other's throats.

Nathan quickly grew accustomed to his aunt and uncle screaming at each other and smashing plates in their rage, but he never ever took to being 'the rat-catcher's boy.'

As the first few weeks of his new life passed, Jago revealed to him that there was much more to his job than simple vermin catching, and what he failed to reveal Nathan was quick to guess for himself. He could tell you, for instance, that if they were called to a better-off house, Jago was sure to map out the rooms, noting their valuables, their best entrances and speediest exits. He would find out where the servants slept or where the dogs lay. He would weaken locks and window-catches. Then it was only a matter of tipping-off his gang, who met regularly at the Duke of Shoreditch pub, and waiting for his share from the break-in. Rarely if ever did Jago himself steal, that was far too risky, but he did sell on stolen goods which were carefully hidden under the cloths of his boat.

As for vermin, Nathan learnt that Jago made free use of the king's licence and saw them in many forms. Mice and rats were all general trade, but Jago was not above taking lawfully owned dogs and cats (which Aunt Maudie skinned, selling the fur to the tailors in Copperpan Street and the meat to a pie seller by the law courts). Nor did it end there. Jago, self-appointed orphan catcher, sold his wretched human captives to the local orphanage, which shamelessly exploited them as unpaid workers in its sweatshops. Nathan grew quite used to frightened urchins fleeing before them like the mice and rats: Jago's name alone enough to clear idle loiterers from street corners like the rumoured approach of a bogeyman.

And all the while Nathan showed no real stomach for any of this. His mother had brought him up respectful and honest and he did not enjoy killing, not even the killing of vermin. Given the slightest opportunity he'd loosen Jago's sack and let the rats go swarming free.

Unlike Nathan's own father when he was alive, Jago liked his drink, and one of Nathan's less unpleasant tasks was to steer Jago safely home from the Duke of Shoreditch, although it meant spending an entire evening in his uncle's company and the company of his equally loathsome gang.

4

At the end of one such evening, when the gin tumblers stood empty on the table between them and one brute was snoring and the others staring vacantly ahead, Jago shoved Nathan with his boot and roared, 'Stir yourself, Nattie boy! Time to take Master Blint home to Bed Land.'

The gang grinned briefly at Nathan, then their expressions slipped back into drunken stupidness, eyes staring, mouths slack.

'Whatever you please, Uncle,' said Nathan blandly.

He rose and dutifully ducked his head under Jago's sweat-stained arm, ready to ease him off the bench. Beneath it he sensed Nip bristle, growling jealously at his closeness to his master. Unsteadily Jago bent down and thrust a hand under the seat.

'Stop your fretting,' he slurred, roughly fondling the dog's ears. 'Don't you know 'tis you I love best of all?'

Ignoring the mild slight, Nathan edged Jago to the door and, with rough farewells bellowed after them, they left the public house in a dense yellow cloud of tobacco smoke and lurched along the darkened alleys, still reeking of it: Jago in a kind of drunken sleep-walk and his dog as close to his heel as possible, faithfully following one crooked step after another.

Jago's cheeks filled with a gassy belch which he gulped down with a hiccup. For a moment or two he stopped walking and his feet were dragged along; when Nathan failed to realize that his uncle wanted him to stop, Jago pushed him aside, taking control of himself once more. Straightening his hat, which had previously sat askew on the back of his head, he swung the four dead mice that hung from it abruptly to attention.

Nathan watched him, seeing some instinct more powerful than rot-gut gin awaken. Curious, he turned and followed his uncle's steady gaze. He saw a boy of roughly his own age lingering uncertainly beneath a gas lamp. The boy kept glancing around as if for landmarks or street signs and in his hand he clutched a leather travelling bag.

'That's 'un as is bound for the orphanage,' muttered Jago beneath his breath.

Nathan looked again. 'But *he's* no ragamuffin, Uncle,' he said. 'There's not a single patch on his clothes and he's wearing *shoes*.'

'He's not one of your regular street-brats, I grant you—but rats, mice, and orphans, I has the Blint gift for sniffing 'em out.'

He began to walk forwards with hardly a stagger, and if it wasn't for the stench of the public house about him, you could hardly tell he had been drinking at all.

'My fine young sir,' he said, greeting the boy with extravagant words and a fulsome smile, 'I have observed you standing here for some time and, if I may say so, with such a puzzled look about you that I says to meself, "That fine young gentleman is lost". May I offer you directions home?'

The boy squinted up his eyes at Jago, judged him sincere and said, 'Well yes, I suppose I am lost, but you can't really direct me home. I don't really have one, you see, sir.'

Jago smiled unpleasantly at Nathan, before putting on an expression of exaggerated sympathy. '*A poor orphan.* May I offer my humble condolences?' His hand rose to doff his hat; the boy stared at the mice.

'You needn't,' he said. 'They died a good many years ago, I hardly knew them.'

'Then you are most likely searching for the house of close relations, sir, who are gladly and bravely raising you like a child of their own?'

'Oh, no,' said the boy carelessly. 'I have no close relatives, either here in the city or anywhere else for that

6

matter. If you insist on helping me, sir, direct me to an affordable lodging-house.'

'*A lodging-house!*' cried Jago, throwing up his hands in dismay. 'A poor orphan alone and friendless in a big city. No—no, I won't hear of it! I insist you pass the night with me and my own poor, humble family, and not a farthing will I accept for my trouble.'

The boy lazily narrowed his eyes, studying Jago more closely. It was clear he did not know what to make of him. Then Nathan saw the boy glance his way and reach a decision.

'Well,' he said, 'that would be uncommonly kind. I am afraid to say my means *are* rather limited.' He stretched out a hand. 'Samuel Hilliam—*Sam* Hilliam— at your service, sir.'

'Jago Blint, your faithful servant and friend, sir. And this wretch at my shoulder'—he gestured at Nathan— 'is Nat, my unfortunate nephew, another orphan I took in out of the goodness of me heart, sir. Generosity, you see, sir, is like a disease as far as I'm concerned, I suffer it fatally.'

Sam nodded at Nathan, whose eyes darted away guiltily. He knew the move made him appear sly, while Jago's sham concerns remained utterly convincing, why, Nathan half believed them himself; and even with the drink inside him, Jago was craftily alive to everything around him. There was no possible way, Nathan realized, he might warn the boy now, the web was spun too tightly around him.

'Come, Master Sam, this way.' Jago swept the boy along and Nathan walked behind, powerless in their shadow.

That night *The Lost Hope* lay moored to a half-collapsed wharf and could only be reached by treading loose timbers that spanned the missing planks. On reaching the canal, Jago lit a lantern previously left hidden on the bankside and held it up for its rays to help Sam see his way across, for the mooring place was as dark as it was silent.

'Pray, young sir, go as careful as you can,' called Jago after him, his voice echoing from tall, unlit flour mills, white with dust as if with newly fallen snow. Nathan stared at his uncle, marvelling at him—why, not half an hour ago he could hardly tell his own left foot from his right.

When Sam safely stepped down on to the boat, Jago roughly pushed Nathan forward, hissing, 'Don't you just stand there. Get after him. We'll put him in your cabin for the night, boy. You can bunk down with your auntie and me.'

Nathan nimbly crossed the wharf and climbed down into the boat. He saw the boy frowning and looking about him, his gaze coming to rest on a nearby metal pipe that was slowly disgorging filth into the canal.

'You live *here*?' he asked in wide-eyed disbelief.

'I know you're probably thinking it's less than what you're used to,' replied Nathan apologetically.

Sam smiled and looked agreeable. 'I don't know—it's much better than anything else I had when you came along and found me.' Then he yawned and stretched.

'See, the young gent is tired, Nattie,' crept Jago's chiding voice over Nathan's shoulder. 'You shouldn't be wearing him out with your mindless babble. This way, sir. You'll find it a most comfortable place to lay your head.'

Hearing voices, Aunt Maudie pushed back the hatches of the main cabin and half emerged on the well deck. She was wrapped in a shawl and a pipe hung crookedly from her mouth. After casting Sam a cold, unconcerned glance she grunted at Jago.

'A good night to you, ma—' began Sam, making to raise his hat.

'Don't you pay her no attention,' said Jago, his voice suddenly hardening, and he gave Sam a shove to make him move further down the boat.

'Ah, here we are,' said Jago. 'Open the hatch for our guest, Nattie. You notice, no door, sir, you go in through the roof.'

'A most sensible arrangement,' said Sam admiringly. 'But, Mr Blint, are you certain I can't give you a penny for my board? I was willing to pay upward of a sixpence . . . '

But Jago wasn't listening. All the while Sam was speaking, Jago was pushing down his head like a jack-in-the-box. Then he slammed down the hatch crying, 'Quick, Nat, get yourself sat on it. I'll fetch some sacks o' coal from the hold to weigh it down.'

Nathan reluctantly obeyed. Beneath him he felt hammering fists.

'I say, Mr Blint—what's happening? I can't seem to get out!'

'Quiet, you young pup,' growled Jago. 'You'll find out all you need to know tomorrow, when I delivers you up at the gates of the orphanage. And don't think that fine leather bag'll accompany you either.'

To Nathan's astonishment Jago had grown slurred again, his soberness as much an act as his friendship, both of which he now saw fit to drop and, after throwing down the last heavy coal sack, he staggered back towards the stern like a man in a hurricane. Swaying for balance, he tied Nip to the tiller then, straightening again, looked around and saw he was alone.

'Come on, Nat,' he roared down the boat. 'He'll be secure enough till morning. Get yourself to bed.'

Nathan heard the clunk of his uncle's boots, carelessly kicked off and discarded on the floor. He gave a violent shiver. Never had he detested his uncle more.

Two

By the time Nathan reached the stern, Jago lay slumped across his bed, face squashed up, mouth gaping and hog-snoring. Aunt Maudie in a furious show of feeling slammed the hatches in Nathan's face and forced him to wait outside until she finished her pipe and gin, which she poured in a dainty fashion from a teapot into a china cup. Shrugging carelessly, Nathan pushed his hands into his pockets and sat beside Nip, who did not wag his tail or try to lick his face, but lay down on his paws with a wary sigh. Nathan knew well that he would not be permitted to enter the cabin until his aunt was decently in bed. He could hear the clink of her cup and saucer; and less frequently, from the bow, came the shouts and hammering fists of the imprisoned boy.

Presently the hammering and shouting stopped for good and Nathan stared purposely towards the silent cabin. Be patient just a little longer, Sam, he thought. I'll do all I can to set you free. I promise, Jago shan't have you like he has me—

Then he started, surprised, because the port-hole nearby had abruptly dimmed. His aunt must have turned out the oil lamp. Lingering a moment or two longer to give her time to pull the covers over herself, Nathan finally stepped down into the cabin, feeling his way through the confined space, the air so thick with tobacco smoke that his eyes smarted. In front of him, behind a drawn curtain, the Blints were bedded, Jago's snores rolling out louder than before. To one side Nathan felt a coarse woollen blanket carelessly tossed on the side bed for him, not that he intended using it. Instead, he sat waiting and listening, leaning towards the curtains drawn across his aunt's and uncle's tiny alcove. After a while he heard Aunt Maudie grind her teeth, angry even in her sleep, and he knew it was safe to slip away.

Cautiously he opened the hatches and Nip was immediately up on his feet, claws scrabbling on the boards. He growled, not with suspicion, but with a deep dislike of the boy.

'Good dog, Nip, it's only me,' whispered Nathan unconvincingly, allowing Nip to sniff his fingers. Nip refused to lie down, but at least he no longer growled.

Making his way quietly to the fore, Nathan arrived at the tiny cabin. He pulled off one of the sacks of coal and crouched down.

'Are you there?' he called as loudly as he dared. 'Master Sam, can you hear me?'

'Of course I can hear you,' replied the boy peevishly. 'Who is it?'

'Nathan—Nathan Wheatear, Jago's orphaned nephew.'

'Well kindly take yourself away, Master Wheatear, so I can plan my escape,' said Sam as if commanding a servant. 'And I shall, you know—escape I mean. You'll not hold me here very much longer—'

'Listen, Sam, I've come to help you, but first I need your promise. If I raise the hatch, do I have your word you'll not make a rush for the opening, but come out as quietly as you can? Trust me and I'll see you safely away from here for ever.'

'Very well,' he heard Sam reply. 'You have my word.'

Nathan quickly pushed aside the three remaining coal sacks, aware of Nip straining on his rope, eagerly watching his every move. He lifted the hatch and Sam's head bobbed up, a lick of hair fallen angrily across his forehead.

The sight of him—the stranger—was like a signal to Nip and he launched into a barrage of furious barking, all the while jumping and twisting and half throttling himself on the end of his short rope. The flour mills echoed back his alarm, until it seemed that he was only one dog among a scrabbling pack, and the two boys believed themselves pursued like foxes. They sped down the boat, Nathan pulling Sam up beside him on to the wharf.

'What's going on out there?' roared Jago, coming out of his drunken sleep like a swimmer fighting his way up through tangled weed.

'Quickly, this way,' hissed Nathan, 'but only put your feet where I do.'

'I can hardly see!' protested Sam.

Nathan crossed the wharf as sure-footed as a sewer rat. Sam followed more hesitantly.

On reaching the bankside they simply turned and ran, trying to lose themselves in the maze of dark alleys, which they did almost immediately, running from one sickly pool of gaslight to the next, the darkness in between stirring as beggars awoke, calling after them for pennies. Nathan grabbed Sam's arm and they ran on, the sound of their footsteps ringing against the barred and shuttered warehouses; while overhead, cranes dangled hooks like hangmans' nooses—or so it seemed in Nathan's wild imaginings; just as the glow of a watchman's lantern in a high window suggested a great sinister eye spying on them for Jago. He was much relieved, therefore, when at last he and Sam burst out on to a wide, brightly lit street, the brick villas reassuringly solid and respectable behind their iron railings. Here Sam pulled him to a standstill.

'Mightn't we stop soon?' he begged.

'Stop?' Nathan looked at him, Sam's face was red and shiny, and his shoulders heaved with each breath.

'Of course . . . I can go on running as long as I like,' said Sam. 'But isn't it rather pointless? Besides . . . we really ought to have a plan by now. I know I'd feel happier with a plan. Look . . . there's a church over the way—just the place for deciding what to do next.'

Nathan glanced across at the darkened church and graveyard. 'You really think we need a plan?' he asked doubtfully.

'You must plan for everything,' said Sam. 'Come on.'

They darted over the road, narrowly avoiding a late-night steam tram that angrily clanged its bell at them. But then at the church's gateway Nathan stopped so abruptly that Sam slammed straight into his back.

'Pooh—you aren't frightened of ghosts and spirits and things, are you?' he said almost mocking. '*I'm* not.'

'But . . . this is St Bartholomew-the-Lesser,' said Nathan. Then he suddenly shut his mouth tight, not wanting to explain that this was the very churchyard where his family lay buried. 'Oh, it's not of any importance,' he added in reply to Sam's look of interest. 'I . . . know this place, that's all.'

A dark, sunken path led to the church and Sam suggested its porch might offer some shelter from the breeze.

'No,' said Nathan firmly. 'We'll go among the gravestones . . . it will give us a clearer view of the road.'

Sam shrugged indifferently and followed Nathan in and out of the many ancient and leaning headstones: and had he been paying better attention, he might have wondered if Nathan was making for a specific place—which of course he was.

'Here,' he said quietly. 'This spot will do.'

He stared down and was ashamed to see the weeds and unkempt grass, while on the stones that marked the graves of his family, tiny growths of moss were beginning to take hold in the deeply chiselled letters.

The two gravestones although white were no longer the unblemished white of new. The larger, grander stone told in the briefest way the histories of his parents; the other much smaller stone for baby Sarah carried just her initials—S. W.—as if she had been too young for proper words.

Casually Sam leaned against the bigger stone and Nathan immediately pulled him off. 'No!' he cried angrily. 'It's disrespectful to the dead.'

'My,' laughed Sam, 'you are a superstitious fellow after all.'

He laid down his bag, straightened, and shot out his hand. Nathan flinched (with good reason, judging by past experiences with Jago) thinking a blow was coming his way. Instead he saw that Sam was smiling gratefully at him. 'You *will* shake?' he asked.

Nathan shook hands and saw Sam give him a curious look. 'Tell me,' he said, 'did your Mr Blint really intend to cart me off to the orphanage?'

'He is not *my* Mr Blint,' replied Nathan coldly. 'And yes, he did. He gets half a crown for every kid he takes to them. None are much like you though.' He was remembering the ragged, wide-eyed waifs who had previously fallen into Jago's clutches. Sam, however, took this for a compliment.

'More fighting spirit, you mean?'

Nathan didn't contradict him.

'Of course,' continued Sam, 'I shouldn't have gone, not to any orphanage, that is. I would have come up with a brilliant plan of escape. I come up with plans of escape all the time, even when I have no need of them. I plan how to escape things like forest fires and cannibals and the direct paths of arrows. It's a gift I have. So I would have escaped your ship eventually—'

'Boat,' corrected Nathan.

'Sorry?'

'On a canal the vessels are called *boats*. Ships go to sea.'

Sam frowned, his expression thoughtful. 'That *is* important, I shall have to remember that,' he said. 'Especially as my plan is to run away to sea.'

Nathan smiled, but then he saw that Sam was deadly serious and Sam was happy to explain why.

'As I told you before, I have no close people of my own,' he said. 'But I do have a guardian, a *Mr Smeasle*.' (It amused Nathan the way he spat out the name, rather like Nathan would say 'Jago Blint', if recounting *his* life story.) 'Mr Smeasle thinks boys an unnecessary luxury,' Sam went on. 'In fact Mr Smeasle thinks bread and cheese an extravagance and lives in a damp, draughty pile in Durham, preferring to suffer chilblains than throw an extra log on the fire. Well, Mr Smeasle manages my affairs and shall do until I reach the age of twenty-one, when he must let me have my inheritance. Meantime, he makes sure that I am brought up with as little expense as possible. That is why I am passing through the city: I'm on my way to Moonville School, some distant, third-rate place that Mr Smeasle's unearthed, where he hopes to have me educated as cheaply as can be done. But I say *Tosh!* to Mr Smeasle. I have made a plan of escape. I mean to see a bit of the world before I come into my money—have an adventure or two. Why, now I come to think of it, I suppose I've had my first adventure already by escaping from your uncle. But I mean to do grander stuff as well.' He clicked his fingers. 'An idea has just come into my head this very instant: I should very much like to visit California and Australia.'

'*California and Australia!* But what about your education?' asked Nathan astonished.

Sam shrugged matter-of-factly. 'Oh, I expect I shall

learn things on the way, you know, useful things like tying knots and how to round the Cape.'

'Still, to miss the chance of going to school and having so many different kinds of books around you.'

'Sounds deadly dull to me,' sniffed Sam.

'Sounds heaven to me,' cried Nathan. 'And it might to you too if you had an aunt like my Aunt Maudie, who threw all my books into the canal the day I went to live with her and Jago. She told me books are as dangerous as snake bites and destroy your eyes. She said anyone with time to sit and read must be idle, but *I* think it the best possible way of passing the time.'

Sam pulled a face. 'It's not fair,' he observed. 'I'd say schools were built for boys like you, while boys like me need to go adventuring.'

They both fell silent for a while, a thought hovering between them—a wildly improbable thought—which first needed Sam to say.

'Look here, Nat,' he began slowly. 'Why not take my place?'

'What?'

'Take my place,' repeated Sam.

Nathan swallowed hard. 'You can't mean—go to school instead of you . . . can you?'

'Why not? Nobody there has the remotest idea of what I look like and Mr Smeasle is never likely to call; better still, it would get you away from your uncle. There, Nat, I have made up a plan of escape for both of us, what a genius I am.'

'No! It's impossible!' cried Nathan. 'It would never work.' Yet despite his words his tone was unsure.

Swept along by his plan, Sam had no time for half-hearted objections. 'It will suit us both exceedingly well,' he said. 'I will write to Smeasle before I set sail asking him to send money which, if he obliges, will be sent to you at school. I, of course, shan't need it by then because I shall be earning a wage as a cabin boy. Oh! it's enough to make a dog laugh, you a scholar and me travelling the world.'

'Slow down, you go too fast!' begged Nathan. 'Aren't you forgetting some important details? Won't I be discovered when the holidays come and you have to return to your guardian?'

Sam grinned broadly. 'Mr Smeasle has made it more than plain he has no wish to set eyes on me until I am sixteen—if then. I am to board on during holiday times.'

'But look at me!' spluttered Nathan. 'I look like a proper guttersnipe and nobody is going to mistake me for anything other.'

Sam picked up the bag and thrust it at him. 'There, it contains the uniform I was supposed to put on, on the way,' he said. 'We're about the same size: I should think it'll fit you no worse than me, though I warn you, it's a horrible scratchy woollen cloth and quite the most disgusting shade of brown. I shan't miss it a bit. Anything else you may need is already sent ahead in a trunk. Well, Nat, what d'you say?'

Nathan opened his mouth to speak but was suddenly confused and made dizzy by such an unlikely offer; if only his parents might somehow tell him what to do. He stared at the white gravestone, willing the dead to speak, and in a way they did, they spoke to him from the past. For wasn't he constantly lectured on the importance of a good education? Didn't his mother sit him on her knee and teach him to read and scratch out his name on a piece of old slate—then all the other words after that? He looked up and saw Sam impatiently waiting for him to decide.

'Very well,' he said, first to himself in a whisper, then: 'Very well, I'll do it! I'll go to school in your place, Sam, I will—*I will*!'

Sam doubled up, laughing. 'What a joke! Old Smeasle paying out for the education of a complete stranger. He hates charity. But it's important to remember, Nat, from this moment on you're no longer Nathan Wheatear, your name is Sam Hilliam.'

'Sam Hilliam,' repeated Nathan, trying on the name like a hat to see how well it fits. He decided it suited him just fine.

'Come on,' said the real Sam, catching his arm. 'There is still time yet. I'll see you aboard your train.'

Before he went, Nathan touched his parents' gravestone for luck, silently wishing for their blessing. Perhaps it wasn't by chance he'd arrived at the churchyard after all.

THREE

Hurrying towards the 'Imp and Salt' (or more correctly the Imperial and Oceanic Railway Terminal), Nathan found his faith in Sam's plan lessening at every step. He realized, as Sam babbled on unendingly about whalers and ice-caps and gold rushes, that his new friend hadn't a realistic notion in his head, just endless waves of enthusiasm and confidence that Nathan had carelessly allowed to sweep him out of his depth. Now, as they rounded a corner, arriving at the square before the great railway station, he was about to discover how fickle Sam was too.

But first, seeing the railway terminal before him, Nathan felt utterly daunted. Slowly his gaze followed the three tiers of steps, with their clusters of cast-iron gas-lamps, up to a solemn building of grand columns and arches; then he tilted his head a little further to take in the roof and the stone mermaid who wore a soldier's helmet and reclined with a smile among the roosting pigeons. Above her fluttered a Union Jack, lit up against the night. In a bewildered daze Nathan followed Sam through the marble booking-halls to the platforms.

Despite the lateness of the hour—an imposing clock hanging from the grimy glass canopy gave it as twenty past midnight—the railway station was buzzing with a huge press of people, and the reason for this was immediately clear. Colonel Crombie's Circus was due to take its leave aboard a specially chartered train, its engine painted red to resemble a dragon and its chimney smoking like the fiery creature's nostrils. Behind the engine, elephants waved their trunks out of high windows like so many dancing cobras, and caravans

19

were being heave-hoed up ramps on to flat trucks. People milled around excitedly: small boys daring each other to lift canvas flaps, catching underneath the green-eyed glint or warning growl of one of the big cats.

The circus folk in their costumes looked wildly glamorous at this late hour—the clowns, the acrobats, the bandsmen, all colourful and glittering. Colonel Crombie himself, a broad, bearded American, wore a fringed deerskin jacket and sat astride a white Spanish stallion, which occasionally he made rear up and pedal the air with its fore hooves to the delight of all who saw.

'Yep,' he was saying in an easy drawl. 'Come straight from performing for her gracious majesty herself, along with so many crowned heads of Europe that, I don't care to boast here, folks, I hadda squint up ma eyes 'gainst the glint of so much jewellery. Was like walking into a blizzard back home in Minnesota. And I tell you, good people, performing at your Crystal Palace was like seeing a glimpse of the future.'

'Why's that?' begged the eager crowd.

'Because,' answered the Colonel, 'the Crystal Palace is so darn big and modern and shiny. And, hey, there ain't no chance of it ever burning down like a big top . . .'

As he spoke nobody paid much attention to the two boys who joined them.

'Look, Nat—look!' whispered Sam, squeezing Nathan's arm in his excitement. 'Imagine what a thing to find at a railway station—a circus. A circus!'

From his very first sighting of it, all thoughts of California and Australia had flown from Sam's mind—indeed, they left in such a rush they might never have lodged there in the first place. The circus, he now decided, was the true and only adventure he had sought all his life.

'But you need to be able to do something,' explained Nathan slowly, as if to a very small child. 'You must be

20

able to juggle, or walk a wire, or take a tumble off a horse.'

'I could be a clown,' said Sam indignantly.

'Joey.'

'What?'

'Clowns call themselves *joeys*.'

'Thanks,' said Sam gratefully. 'That is something useful I'll need to know.'

Nathan sighed. Sam's boundless confidence was exhausting—it was like trying to control a puppy-dog. 'But even joeys have skills they must learn,' he said.

He saw Sam frown and knew him to be thinking. When the frown disappeared and he again smiled in that charming way of his, Nathan guessed that the thought had run its course.

'Where are you going?' he called as Sam brushed past him. Sam did not reply but marched purposely towards one of Colonel Crombie's richly carved show-wagons, which was decorated with 'Scenes of the Empire'— jungles, temples, and wild creatures terrifying natives— along with countless flags and pieces of diamond-shaped mirror. Before Nathan could stop him he began to climb up the side.

'Sam! Sam! Come down at once, you idiot, before you land us both in trouble.'

Sam, however, now stood on the wagon's roof, hands on hips, surveying the jostle of toppers, bonnets, and bowlers below, as if from the top of a mountain.

'Colonel Crombie!' he called. 'Oh, Colonel Crombie, sir.'

The big American lifted his eyes, along with everyone else who heard him call. There were giggles and amused smiles, but not from Colonel Crombie himself—Colonel Crombie wrinkled up his brow.

'Excuse my impertinence, Colonel Crombie, sir,' continued Sam, 'but I beg to ask a favour of you.

21

Allow me, sir, to join your excellent circus. If you do I'll gladly travel anywhere in the whole world with you.' He spoke with such simplicity and charm that Nathan thought it must be difficult for anyone to refuse him anything.

Colonel Crombie, however, was unmoved. 'We don't take on no runaways,' he growled.

'But I'm not a runaway,' protested Sam. 'I'm an orphan.'

The word *orphan* magically brought the crowd on to his side, particularly the ladies.

'He's a good-looking boy,' commented someone.

'What can you do, son?' enquired someone else.

'I can sing, sir,' replied Sam. 'And if you employ me, Colonel, I promise to sing every night with your band.'

There and then, despite the bustle and the hissing trains and the porters who bawled at each other across the tracks, he began to sing. In truth the song he chose was a mawkish thing about always loving your mother, and bees sucking nectar, and returning to the home fire after a long absence; but his voice carried over the heads of the multitude, amplified by the curve of the great glass roof. Gradually other voices subsided, movement grew still. Porters stood gazing dumbly, and engine-drivers and firemen leaned black-faced from their cabs. He had such a sweet voice that it made Nathan quite envious to hear it, especially when he noticed one or two around him dab their eyes. Then Nathan grinned to himself. The circus was a natural place for Sam—he understood perfectly how to milk an audience.

The song ended, Sam's voice drifted away into the station's furthest corners and the spell was broken. A moment later the crowd responded with thunderous applause, scattering the pigeons at roost among the iron beams.

'Well, Colonel?' demanded the assembled. 'Shall you give the boy a go?'

Colonel Crombie shrugged. 'Aw, I dun' know. He sure has a showman's style and his voice ain't so bad either. But I dun' know.'

Just then Caspar Nagel, circus strongman, burst through the crowd. He wore a real leopard skin over a pair of pink long-johns and his eyes glistened with sentimental tears. Now Caspar was a big ox-like Bavarian with muscles that could, and did, snap iron chains, but his heart couldn't have been softer had it been stuffed with goose feathers.

'The boy, he must be with the show, Herr Ringmaster,' he sniffed. 'He is a' orphan und he sing like a' angel. I tell you, he can live with my frau un' I in our caravan. But say first he is permitted to join your circus, Herr Ringmaster, jus' say he is.'

'We-ll,' drawled the Colonel, scratching under his hat. 'Guess you've kinda decided the matter for me, Caspar.' And half rising in the saddle he announced, 'Ladies and gentlemen, Colonel Crombie's travelling circus proudly presents its latest sen-sational discovery. May I in-tro-duce to you the fabulous, the stu-pendous s-ing-ing orphan boy!'

'Hooray!' responded the crowd, raising their hats as high as their voices, as Sam was led away on the strongman's shoulders, beaming and waving as if he had been a circus performer all his life.

Nathan was afraid this would be the last he saw of his friend. The crowd swallowed him up faster than quicksand and gradually Nathan got jostled to its edge. Away from the centre of things, a sour kind of disappointment built up inside him, leaving him close to tears; and he almost felt angry at Sam for filling his head with such ripe nonsense, which Jago, no doubt, would knock clean out of him again—

'Hey!'

The shout came from the crowd and Nathan's whole face suddenly lit up. 'Sam!' he whooped.

'No, not Sam, you idiot,' said his friend, who was wearing a bandsman's cap several sizes too large for him. '*You're Sam Hilliam*, remember?' He struggled against a surge of people. 'It took me an age to find you. Here, I forgot to give you this.' He handed Nathan a railway ticket. 'Third class I'm afraid, but that's our Mr Smeasle for you. Now you must hurry. Platform 2A. The train leaves in five minutes—oh, you must remember to get off at Humphton and ask for directions to the school.'

'Humphton,' repeated Nathan, gasping out his thanks.

Sam grinned. 'Only returning the favour. Shake?'

This time Nathan shook the offered hand readily and warmly.

'Now go,' said Sam. 'And good luck, although I expect you'll turn out to be a dry old professor covered in ink blots, with quills stuck in your hat like a Red Indian chief.'

He pushed Nathan to get him moving; Nathan turned and waved at him, still unable to believe that any of this was happening.

'Don't miss your train!' mouthed Sam, adding: 'And I'll write to Smeasle on your behalf. Don't worry, he's too mean to buy new spectacles so he won't notice the strange postmark.'

Nathan nodded and hurried away, following the signs to platform 2A, where a little chocolate-brown tank engine stood with three coaches behind it, quite dull compared to the circus express, but Nathan felt drunk with happiness seeing it there for him. The world, which only that morning had been so solid and grey, had been pulled from underneath his feet like a carpet and it felt as if he was tumbling head first into something utterly different and undreamt of—

Then all at once the world swung back to how it used to be. Under the great entrance arch, glaring at him with wild, red eyes, stood Jago, the dead mice around his hat provoking looks of disgust from those who were forced to walk around him. From his hand ran a length of rope with Nip on the end straining to be let loose.

Before he could prevent it, a cry escaped from Nathan's mouth, and his heart swelled and thudded in his chest. He knew that if he didn't turn and run, Jago's glare would freeze him to the spot. Gripping the leather bag, he fled down the platform, clumsy at every step and almost tripping in his panic. Sweat tingled on his brow. When he came to the train he fumbled with the door of the nearest carriage, but it was as if his fingers had lost their strength and he was quite unable to open it.

'Here, let me help you, sir,' said a porter, opening it with ease.

Nathan hardly noticed him there and seizing the strap handle slammed the door shut behind him and sat with his back pressed against a hard, wooden seat. Then he found *not* knowing worse than knowing, so he forced himself to gaze out of the window.

As steadily as something in a nightmare, Jago was making straight towards him, pushing aside any obstacle in his path and even knocking one man clean on to his back.

'Oh, please, no,' whispered Nathan, gripping his knees. So distraught was he that he didn't notice the shrill whistle blown right outside his window; and he believed he was shaking from head to foot, such was the terror he felt for his uncle. Only then he realized he wasn't shaking at all: it was merely the roll of the train as it started out on its journey.

He flew to the window a second time and saw Jago break into a run, almost pulled off his feet by the slavering terrier. The carriage was quickly gathering speed, but Jago was faster and nearly alongside it. Nathan heard his uncle's fingers desperately scrabbling against the door for the handle.

'Damn you! You'll not escape as easily as you think, Nathan Wheatear.'

Suddenly Jago's roar was cut dead—left behind along with the brightly lit station and all its people, as the little train slipped into the darkness at the end of the platform.

Sitting very still until he was calm, Nathan whispered to himself, 'No, not Nathan Wheatear . . . *My* name is Sam Hilliam.'

FOUR

Soon the train settled to a regular speed, swaying with a reassuring thrum. Never in all his life had Nathan travelled anywhere by railway before and now, despite an unnerving departure and an uncertain end, he meant to enjoy this part of his journey at least. A single oil lamp in the ceiling gave a poor, shadowy light, and by it Nathan gazed around at the empty wooden seats. With no fellow passengers to tut or stare disapprovingly he was free to sit wherever he pleased. He chose the seat by a small window, which he opened as wide as it would go, letting the night wind rush through his hair, tasting the gritty smuts thrown up with each puff of smoke.

Outside lay the city with its back to him and lit up with gas lamps; and sometimes, if he stared hard enough, Nathan had the giddy sensation that *he* was the one standing perfectly still and it was the city that moved. But at other times it seemed to him that the city was more like a guide-book, its pages flicking by so swiftly that, in the space of a few seconds, he had gone from mansions to slums, from markets to churches, from hospitals to graveyards . . .

And then into a tunnel.

Emerging with a screaming whistle on its far side, Nathan was surprised to see not a single brick of the city remained and the train passed unnoticed through dark, flat countryside.

Nathan opened the leather bag.

It was time for him to change.

He took off his clothes and quickly dressed himself in Sam's school uniform, finding it cut a little on the large side (Mr Smeasle obviously counting on growth before wear), but everything had the glorious smell of newness about it. The trousers and jacket were itchy as Sam had warned, but the waistcoat was dark red silk and sent Nathan several times to the window to admire his reflection. It was a pity, however, that he had to make do with his old, scuffed boots; and his dirty finger-nails brought on a flush of shame, remembering his mother who used to keep an entire cupboard for her blocks of carbolic soap. For a while he tried spit and polish but his mouth was too dry from nervousness, besides which nothing he did made any real difference because the grime had become a part of him, so he cat-licked his hair flat and sat absolutely still, desperately trying not to wrinkle his new clothes.

'Sam Hilliam.'

He suddenly spoke the name to the empty carriage, saying it over and over to hear if it sounded better now that he was dressed for the part.

'Sam Hil-li-am.'

Convinced and pleased that it did, he snoozed through the next three station stops.

It was very late when the train finally pulled into Humphton station. Nathan got up and left his old clothes behind like a snake discarding its skin: he just picked up the empty leather bag and stepped out on to the platform, into a cloud of hissing steam. Through it he glimpsed a round, smiling face.

'Just let me see the train on her way, sir, and I'll attend to you directly.'

Nathan's voice clogged his throat. He managed a nod. The man blew a whistle and the train chugged out of the station.

Feeling oddly exposed, Nathan hooked one scuffed boot behind the other, standing awkwardly like a stork on one leg.

The man hurried back a little out of breath and eased the ticket from Nathan's tense fingers.

'You the young gent bound for the school?' he asked. Nathan gave a second expressionless nod.

'We were expecting you yesterday, sir,' said the man, cheerful enough for the both of them. 'I'm Rabbitson, the stationmaster: well, stationmaster, ticket seller, porter, and all round odd-job man.' He removed his stationmaster's cap. 'I can take your bag if you like, sir, now I'm no longer stationmastering . . . Oh, you do travel light, sir, if I may say so.'

Mr Rabbitson led Nathan to his comfortable house nearby. It was lit with red, softly glowing railway lamps, and on the walls instead of pictures were timetables because Mr Rabbitson believed nothing was so beautiful as a well run railway. In the parlour he riddled the dying coals back to flame.

'You sit yourself down there, sir,' he told Nathan, ushering him towards a fireside chair. 'Make yourself at home; why, you won't be able to reach your new school this time of night, sir, so you best get by on Rabbitson's hospitality.'

He put a kettle on the fire for tea, but before the water had boiled, Nathan—comfortable and warm—had fallen fast asleep.

Nathan's eventful day unwound like a giant spring in his head. As he slept he dreamt of circuses, station crowds, and rushing buildings, each dream scene filling him with happiness—until Jago appeared. A mean, scowling face in the distance, pushing to the fore—

Nathan awoke with a sharp intake of breath and found himself in the stationmaster's chair with a blanket thrown over him. Mr Rabbitson was bending low, his face close to his own.

'Sorry, sir,' he said. 'Didn't mean to startle you, but

we best be on our way. I've the pony and trap at the door ready to run you up to Moonville. George can see off the 8.17.'

'Thank you,' said Nathan, amazed to find it already morning.

Mr Rabbitson took his bag and fussed over him in a way Nathan supposed all gentlemen were fussed over because he never knew the like before, but he refused the stationmaster's offer of bread and jam, feeling too nervous to swallow a single crumb.

Outside he was helped up on to the trap and Mr Rabbitson took the driving seat. With a flick of the reins and click of the tongue they set off.

Much of the journey passed unnoticed by Nathan and the sights Mr Rabbitson carefully pointed out to him went unremembered afterwards. He felt sick with apprehension. What would he discover? How would he be treated? More importantly, what if he were found out? *What indeed?*

Thirty minutes later the stationmaster pulled up the pony. 'Here we are then, sir—your new school.'

Slowly Nathan turned to see.

Through an iron gateway, beyond a circular gravel drive, stood a low, rambling building with a buckled roof and an extravagant number of tall chimneys. At one end loomed a gloomy, forbidding tower which seemed to have little to do with the rest of the building—almost managing to turn its back on it. And while the tower had narrow slots in its thick walls, the main block had many small leaded windows. From one, a calico shirt was hung out to dry, being the only evidence that anyone lived there—apart from the swooping house martins whose little mud nests thronged the eaves like barnacles upon a ship's hull.

When Nathan showed no sign of moving, Mr Rabbitson gently cleared his throat. 'You best climb

30

down now, sir. Don't want to miss the 9.18, do I?' He patted Nathan's hand in a fatherly way. 'I'm sure you'll do your best, sir.'

Stumbling and awkward, Nathan got down from the trap and mumbled his thanks and goodbyes as Mr Rabbitson wheeled the pony around and headed back to the station.

When he was gone, Nathan carried his empty bag across to the gate and peered through the bars like a condemned prisoner. And, as he stood there wishing he was somewhere else, a dormer window flew open and a boy leaned out squinting down the barrel of a shotgun. Taking aim in Nathan's general direction he immediately fired.

The explosive sound was accompanied by a cloud of blue smoke.

Nathan, startled, leapt into a bush.

FIVE

'*Sorry.*'

The apologetic boy peered deep into the bush. He still held the shotgun, which smelt of fresh powder-smoke, but its barrel pointed harmlessly to the ground. Nathan blinked back at him, suddenly feeling rather foolish.

'I didn't mean to frighten you,' continued the boy. 'I saw this pigeon, you see, and I simply couldn't resist taking a shot at it.'

'Did you hit it?' enquired Nathan from within his bush.

'What?'

'Did you hit the pigeon?'

'Heavens, no,' roared the boy. 'Rotten shot. Still, it doesn't stop me from trying. You must be the new boy—leastways, you look very new. Here, let me help you out, it can't be very pleasant in there with all those spiders and things.'

Nathan took his hand and emerged from cover with bits of twig and dead leaf in his hair.

'Tadcaster,' beamed the boy. 'Richard Tadcaster—Richie to m' friends.'

'Er, Sam Hilliam,' replied Nathan, his tongue nearly tripping on the shameless lie.

Richie beamed again and picked a piece of bush off Nathan's sleeve. Nathan saw that Richie was dressed in a grubby nightshirt, mended with numerous patches; from the knees down he was bare legged.

'Are you ill?' asked Nathan, and supposing this to be the answer was already sympathetic.

'Heavens, no,' said Richie amused. 'At Moonville no boy stirs from bed much before ten o'clock. Lucky for you I saw you when I did or you would have knocked on the door until your knuckles bled. Are you hungry? Heavens, I always am. Come on, let's find something to eat.'

He led the way through the gate to the school, the building seeming to grow before Nathan's eyes, spreading out and becoming more rambling.

'It looks fairly ancient,' he whispered in awe. 'How old is it?'

'Lor', don't ask me,' replied Richie. 'I'm a complete duffer when it comes to dates. I say the only two dates worth a boy's notice are his birthday and Christmas. When's your birthday, Sam?'

Taken by surprise by this simple question, Nathan didn't know whether to answer for himself or the real Sam Hilliam, whose birthday was unknown to him in any case. 'Oh . . . oh, my b-birthday?' he stammered. 'N-not yet, I'd say—perhaps soon.'

He was so annoyed with himself that he pinched his leg through his pocket. In future he must learn to be on his guard against simple slip-ups like this.

Richie grinned. 'Never mind, let's hope you're better at remembering Christmas. Right, here we are, come on in.'

He opened the main door, which was heavy and studded in iron, into a dark hall with a passage beyond and a gloomy stairway rising along one wall. The oaken panelling was as antique as anything outside, but Nathan stared at it in astonishment seeing that boys had carved their names and initials deep into the wood (some using elaborate capitals or scrolling tails) and each inscription had a date carved alongside.

Mistaking Nathan's reason for lingering, Richie said, 'Oh, don't bother yourself with that now, Sam, you can come back and scratch your name at any old time. Borrow my penknife if you like, it's the best in school.'

He walked towards a set of double doors. 'In here is the most important place in the whole building,' he said grandly. 'The refectory. It's where us starving boys get given the swill that passes for our daily grub.'

Another surprise awaited Nathan behind the doors, which opened into what must have been the old house's Great Hall.

Long tables and forms ran its length to a raised platform at the end, where a finer table was surrounded by individual chairs (Nathan rightly guessing that this was where the masters sat, for it gave a clear view of the floor below).

None of this was unusual in any way—but what set Nathan's eyebrows soaring was the spectacular mess. A meal, presumably last night's supper, lay uncleared away and everywhere he looked Nathan saw sticky blobs of food, upturned bowls, and spoons left tossed upon the floor; several benches lay upside down surrounded by bread, bones, and squashed potatoes, and buttery hand-prints glistened on the walls. A pool of spilt water, having made a rivulet to the end of the table, dripped steadily on to the tiles—which appeared in need of a good wash in any case. Carefully edging around a pile of boiled cabbage, Nathan paused to gaze up at an old-fashioned portrait of a well-to-do man, which should have been high enough to be out of harm's way, yet in the centre of the picture, deeply embedded into his nose were the prongs of a well-aimed fork. No wonder the fellow glowered down at him! As to the ornate ceiling, this was so peppered with gun-shot that in places it resembled the wormiest timbers of an ancient church.

All these details took a while to take in. When Nathan again turned to Richie, he saw him drifting between tables, finding an odd crust here and there and cramming it into his mouth, without the slightest pretence of manners. Feeling hungry all of a sudden

Nathan did exactly the same and they shared a bottle of flat beer together.

'You best go present yourself at Beefy's house next,' Richie informed him.

'Who's Beefy?' asked Nathan, draining the last of the beer.

Richie frowned and took the bottle from him, checking it was really empty before setting it down. 'Heavens,' he said, 'don't you know anything? Beefy is the headmaster of this rot-hole prison for boys. *Boscombe Bentbeef*. A word of warning though, never lend him any money. The old devil still owes me sixpence from last Shrove Tuesday.'

He looked around but saw there was nothing left to eat or drink, so he scratched under his arm and yawned noisily. Nathan got to his feet.

'Thanks, Richie,' he said. 'Will you answer me one last question if I promise not to ask any more?'

'I might,' said Richie.

'Where do I find Mr Bent—I mean *Beefy*'s house?'

'You must have passed it on your way up with Rabbitson,' said Richie, breaking off to yawn again. 'Heavens, I really think I ought to go back to bed and finish off my nap. Good luck with Beefy, Sam, and remember, don't lend him a single penny.'

Reaching the double doors, Nathan turned to see that Richie had laid his head upon the table; his eyes were shut and his hair was sticking to a splodge of jam.

Mr Bentbeef's house stood a little way apart from the school, behind a neat, well-ordered garden and although old was by no means as old as the school. At its gate Nathan hesitated. He wondered if Mr Bentbeef was as late to rise as his boys. The house appeared very quiet, so Nathan wandered up and down the lane six or seven times before daring to approach the door and tug the bell-pull. At the back of the house arose an insistent jangle and immediately and violently the door was yanked open by a skinny young maid.

'Too hard! Too hard!' she snapped, vigorously polishing the bell-pull to rid it of Nathan's fouling fingerprints.

Nathan took several steps backwards. 'G-good morning,' he said. 'I'm Hilliam . . . the new boy—here to report to Mr Bentbeef.'

The maid bobbed up on her toes, peering over and around his head, down the length of the garden. 'You hain't been picking the flowers has you? Or treading them down?'

'Certainly not,' said Nathan.

'So why were you loitering by 'em and eyeing 'em up so? I sees yer. Those flowers are Mrs Bentbeef's flowers they are, every last one o' 'em.'

Nathan assured her he wasn't in the least interested in Mrs Bentbeef's flowers, not that the maid seemed convinced.

'Well, wipe your feet if you're coming in,' she said fiercely, standing narrowly aside to let him pass. 'You best wait in the study.'

'Mr Bentbeef's study?' asked Nathan innocently.

'*Mr Bentbeef's study*,' snorted the maid, scornfully blowing out her cheeks. 'Mr Bentbeef's *nothing*!'

She opened the study door, her hand covered by her apron so as not to mark the shiny brass handle.

'Stand here, Hilliam,' she commanded, pointing to an exact spot by the edge of the rug, but definitely not on it. 'And don't dare fidget or touch anythin',' she growled.

She glanced him up and down one last time, sniffed disapprovingly and marched out to find Mr Bentbeef. As soon as she had gone, Nathan let out his breath and stopped standing so rigidly to attention. Cautiously he looked around.

Unlike the parts of the school he had seen, the study was neat, clean and smelt of recent polish; silver, gilt, and crystal glinted and the piano glowed a rich mahogany. The room was also smartly wall-papered and at the windows swags of heavy plum velvet and Nottingham lace dimmed the morning light.

Yet only when Nathan considered the room's appearance quite ordinary did he begin to notice things that were not so. Like the two framed embroideries above the fireplace. 'MY home sweet home', read the first; 'Breakages must be paid for', read the second. Both were handsomely worked in silk thread, and interweaving the hostile words were brightly coloured birds, butterflies, and flowers.

Equally as odd, now Nathan came to think about it, were the tiny white labels threaded to every object in the room, from a candle-snuffer to the piano itself. Daring to catch one, he turned it over in his fingers and read: 'Exclusive property of Mrs B.'

Before he could ponder on what this might mean, he heard raised voices in the hall and quickly sprang back to attention on his appointed spot.

'I demand you always address me with a civil tongue, Rose,' insisted a man petulantly. 'D'you hear? Civil! And a "sir" and a curtsy now and again wouldn't go amiss either.'

And there in the doorway stood Mr Bentbeef, much agitated, straightening his mortarboard and gown (yet not before Nathan had caught sight of the potato and gravy stains upon his crumpled waistcoat). He was a short, florid man, whose squint gave him a permanently worried expression—or perhaps it was that his worried expression gave him a permanent squint.

'*Hmmph.*' He realized Nathan was listening and shrugged his threadbare gown a final time. 'Ah yes. Hilliam. You were expected yesterday, boy.'

'Sorry, sir,' replied Nathan, adding slyly, 'I had an unexpected change on the journey.'

'No matter—no matter,' said Mr Bentbeef, carelessly waving his hand. 'You are safely here now.'

He crossed to a green leather armchair and sank heavily into it, gathering up his gown around him with a flourish as he sat. The bottoms of his shoes revealed two large holes, which he made no attempt to hide.

'Well come, sir. Stand before me now I am here.'

Nathan did so, but remembering the cross maid preferred to edge around the rug rather than walk directly over it.

Mr Bentbeef peered deep into Nathan's face. 'To tell you the truth, Hilliam, I half expected you to have horns.'

'Horns, sir?' Nathan looked puzzled.

'Why yes—and a pointed tail.'

'Like a devil, sir?' said Nathan.

'A devil indeed, Hilliam. It's all to do with this letter I received from your guardian. I have it about me somewhere.' He searched inside his gown, found it, and held it closely before his eyes. 'A Mr Smeasle, who writes . . . yes, here it is . . . that you are "lazy, conceited and lacking in the most basic of discipline." Tut-tut. We can't have that, Hilliam. Not at Moonville. Here we are in the business of heddication. We take a dull boy and make him shine. Yes—yes. Like a new penny, Hilliam . . . or a shilling . . . or better still, a g-olden sovereign. Tell me—tell me,' said the headmaster growing more animated. 'Have you ever held a brand new sovereign in your hand and felt the thrrrob of our noble currency? Oh, the joy of it, Hilliam, the endless possibilities of an unspent coin, the—'

Here his heroic flow of words was suddenly cut short by the door flying open and a furious woman in a black poke bonnet storming in (Mrs Bentbeef undoubtedly,

38

tipped off by Rose the maid). She glared about her, her eyes eventually resting their burning beams on the seated bulk of her husband.

'Bentbeef!' she roared, clenching up her fists. 'What mean you by this, sir? Who gave you leave to plonk yourself in me chair? Get yourself up orf and away from it this instant. D' y' hear?'

And Mr Bentbeef, dropping the letter, leapt clean out of the chair as though he were sitting on a bag of red hot farthings.

SIX

Nathan and Mr Bentbeef managed to flee the house only after Mr Bentbeef had been chased several times around the room, his wife screaming the most dreadful insults at him. Rose stood in the hall ready with the front door open, then slammed it on their heels as they made their escape. In the garden, Mr Bentbeef took off his mortarboard and mopped his brow and neck with a handkerchief, and apart from 'Unfortunate . . . unfortunate' made no further mention of his wife's furious outburst.

Nathan was shocked, but not having a wide knowledge of schools saw no reason to suppose this wasn't typical behaviour. Only later did he learn why Mrs Bentbeef took so violently against her husband. In her eyes he was a worthless head of an inadequate school, weighed down by debt and pursued by a growing army of creditors. While she, on the other hand, was a woman of independent wealth, with a handsome allowance from her aged father. Since most things in the house belonged to her, the little white tags were her way of constantly pointing this out. And while she lived in comfort, Mr Bentbeef was reduced to dining on cold scraps in the kitchen and sleeping in a cupboard under the stairs.

'Come, Hilliam, we must attend to your schooling,' said Mr Bentbeef, recovered enough to sound brisk. 'But look here, before we do, I'm afraid I'm a little short at the moment. You couldn't see your way clear to lending me half a crown? How about a shilling then?'

Nathan shook his head. But had he the money in his pocket he certainly would have given it to him—if only out of pity.

40

'Ah well,' sighed Mr Bentbeef and they walked up the lane together.

As they approached it, Nathan saw signs that the school had at last awoken. Windows and doors were open to air various rooms and the drone of voices floated his way. Inside, it was no better than before, not that Mr Bentbeef appeared to notice: hitching up his gown he stepped nimbly over an axe stuck deep into the floorboards and reached out to open a door.

'Pay heed, Hilliam,' he said. 'Your future classroom.'

Following him through the doorway, Nathan saw some twenty boys aged from seven to thirteen, sitting in silent rows facing a tall youth of about eighteen, who stood slouched over a reading-desk. He turned his sleepy, half-closed eyes towards Nathan and a languid smile appeared. About his neck he wore a flamboyant, floppy bow and his waistcoat was brightly coloured with a multitude of little embroidered birds. Over his collar his blond hair threw a curl or two, and there was an easy grace about him which Nathan immediately liked.

He was—or so it appeared—engaged in teaching.

'Bunk

Bunk-off

Bunk-up

Bunk-um,' he intoned.

'Bunk

Bunk-off

Bunk-up

Bunk-um,' the boys chanted back. Then the youth pretended to be surprised at finding Mr Bentbeef standing close by.

'Ah, Mr Bentbeef, good morning, sir. You honour us with your presence.' His words were extravagant and mocking at the same time. All the other boys immediately rose, their forms scraping upon the wooden floor.

41

'Keeping 'em busy, eh, Lavender?'

'Latin, Mr Bentbeef. Irregular verbs. Endless, tedious stuff, sir.'

'Splendid . . . splendid. Remember what I've told you. Heddication should be like medicine—if it ain't nasty it's doing 'em no good.'

Lavender smiled. 'Believe you me, sir, this is pure castor oil.'

Mr Bentbeef paced up and down, resolutely playing the headmaster, his hands tucked behind him beneath his gown.

Then he stopped and pointed at a small, quaking boy whose hair stood on end. 'You, sir, do you say your prayers every night?'

'Y-yes, s-sir. Every n-night.'

'And do you include your mother and father in your prayers?'

'Y-yes, s-sir.'

'Good . . . good. And you, sir,'—to a boy at the back—'what is known as the sport of kings?'

'Horse racing, sir,' answered the boy.

'Indeed it is . . . indeed it is. And you, sir, what is the capital of France?'

After a painful silence the third boy stammered, 'D-don't know, sir.'

Mr Bentbeef sprang up and down on his toes before him. 'Don't know, sir. *Don't know*. Nor why should you! Load of Frenchie nonsense if you ask me.'

He turned briskly on his heels to face Lavender again. 'Brought you a new boy—Hilliam. Keep him to his lessons, sir, and make sure he doesn't go astray. He's a full boarder and these days full boarders are better than gold in me teeth.'

'I understand *perfectly*, Mr Bentbeef, sir,' replied Lavender, and Nathan felt Lavender's amused eye fall directly on him.

'Good . . . good. Now on with your verbing, boys!'
Mr Bentbeef went striding towards the door, but once
there he paused and turned back as if remembering
something. 'Oh, and Lavender . . . if there happens to
be any frog racing today, be good enough to place a
couple o' shillings on Pond Boy for me.'

Lavender grimaced. He knew Mr Bentbeef had no
intention of paying for his bet, but would fully expect
any winnings.

With a contented smile on his face, Mr Bentbeef
sailed out of the room and the boys relaxed noticeably.
Lavender tweaked Nathan's ear.

'Who will volunteer to take this evil loathsome little
brat off my hands?' he asked in a tone of affected
boredom.

The boys responded by pelting Nathan with a volley
of paper balls.

'Leave it to me, Lavender,' called a voice. 'I'll show
him the ropes.' And Nathan was glad to see Richie (now
fully dressed) grinning across at him. 'Come sit by me,
Sam,' he said. 'You mustn't mind Lavender, he's going
to die soon.'

'Is he ill?' asked Nathan shocked.

'Ill? Lor' no. What a thing you have with illness, Sam.
Lavender wants to be a poet and he says all the best
ones die young.'

Glancing across at Lavender, who had taken a leg of
cold chicken from his desk and was biting into it,
Nathan couldn't imagine anyone less likely for an early
grave.

Something else puzzled him too. 'What did Beefy
mean about *frog racing*?' he asked.

Richie rolled his eyes. 'There you go, asking questions
again,' he said. 'Just sit tight for a bit longer and you'll
find out all you want to know, they'll be bound to be
under starter's orders soon—'

43

He broke off suddenly as a shoe came flying through the air. He ducked, Nathan didn't, and the shoe hit him on the nose.

'Oh, bad luck,' said Richie.

As Nathan rubbed his nose, trying to regain his dignity, he looked about him, hardly able to believe this the same class as he had entered a few minutes ago. Boys sat with their feet up on desks, smoking pipes or drinking ale; some were playing cards or dozing with their heads nestled in their arms. But these boys were the few—the rest were all too ready to squabble or wrestle upon the floor and afterwards hang the loser upside-down by his ankles. The noise was worse than a rowdy tavern. Nobody spoke when he could roar, and nobody walked between desks when he might go running across their tops. A boy called Ducksfoot leaned from the window to retrieve Molly, a small piglet, to which he was devoted and which went everywhere with him tucked inside his coat; and Molly contributed to the commotion with squeals and grunts.

No attempt was made at teaching and Lavender, tossing his chicken bone over his shoulder, banged a desk and announced, 'Gentlemen, it's time again. Let the frog Derby begin!'

A cheer rang out, but at least afterwards there was a little more order. First the blackboard was turned around, revealing the names of different frogs and their betting odds. Then the frogs themselves were brought out, squirming and slippery and clumsily held in the boys' hands, the favourites much admired. The race course ran from the front of the class to the back and the boys crowded eagerly along it.

'Silence, you wretched savages!' bellowed Lavender, and when their voices dwindled away he turned to Nathan and said, 'Hilliam, it is my dubious pleasure to welcome you to your first frog Derby. I'd wish you luck if I didn't need it all for myself. Now speak up and tell us on which of these fine creatures will you put your money?'

'But . . . ' Nathan felt his face redden, knowing he hadn't a farthing to his name.

Pennington, a lanky boy with very pale skin and hair so blond you could see his pink scalp through it, noticed him hesitate. 'Perhaps the new boy doesn't bet, Lavender,' he sneered. 'Or perhaps he is a pauper. Look at his boots—no better than a common workman's if you ask me.'

'Oh shut up, Pennington,' said Lavender, crushing him with a glance.

Just then Nathan felt Richie slip a coin into his hand and smiled his thanks.

He studied the names on the blackboard.

'A penny on Tadpole Terror,' he said decisively.

SEVEN

By the end of his first day, Nathan no longer felt quite so guilty for having taken on Sam Hilliam's identity. It was hardly fraud, he reasoned, when the school was just as big a fake as he was, for in all his time there he never once glimpsed a book or wetted a nib with ink. Smoking, wrestling, and frogs appeared to be the boys' main subjects and were taken up with a passion rarely associated with arithmetic and geography.

Still, Nathan was uneasy at having to mislead his new friend Richie, for without Richie to guide him through the complex, often mysterious ways of school life, he would have been lost. More than once Richie stopped him from making a complete fool of himself, and Nathan was very glad to have at least one ally throughout the riots that at Moonville passed themselves off as meal times.

Having survived supper, Richie offered to help Nathan carry his large wooden trunk up to the dormitories: the things of the real Sam Hilliam were so heavy that at every landing the two boys paused for breath.

'What on earth have you stashed away in here?' asked Richie, as they started up the next flight.

'Haven't a clue, I didn't pack it,' answered Nathan truthfully. 'Oh, don't slow down again, Richie, we'll never reach the top of the stairs at this rate.'

'I have to,' sulked Richie. 'I'm not your pack-horse, you know.'

As they paused with the trunk propped up between them, a loud commanding voice said, 'Step aside and be quick about it, I'm coming through.'

Nathan looked up sharply to catch sight of that unpleasant tall boy who had tried to belittle him in class that morning.

'Go round, can't you, Pennington,' replied Richie coldly. 'Can't you see we're struggling? Better still, you can lend us a hand.'

Pennington stared at him in disbelief at the very suggestion. 'Why should I? I have better things to do with my time than waste it rescuing penniless brats. Move aside, I say; a Pennington goes round no one.'

With that he gave Richie a shove. Richie yelped, almost losing balance and falling backwards. Just in time he grabbed the carved bannister, but as soon as he let go of the trunk's front end it tipped back, landing on Nathan's foot then, unable to stop, it crashed down every step to the previous landing. Fearing it might run away completely, Nathan raced after it and sat on the lid, panting for breath. Pennington came down smirking to himself.

'Perhaps you should have taken the servants' stairs,' he suggested sarcastically.

Nathan leapt up. 'And perhaps you need to be taught a lesson in manners,' he replied.

For the flicker of a moment Pennington was taken aback by Nathan's fierceness, but then he was amused. Not only was Nathan noticeably smaller than himself but also a good year younger. How his smile infuriated Nathan, who knew exactly what he thought.

'Manners come from breeding, not teaching,' said Pennington loftily and he pushed Nathan too. Had he not stood prepared for it, Nathan would have fallen clean over the trunk. His anger renewed, he hurled himself at Pennington and together they crashed down on to the landing—brawling—meeting each other blow for blow, Pennington's strength evenly matched by Nathan's fury.

'Sam . . . Sam!' squawked Richie, unable to separate them, and Nathan too maddened to notice him.

In the strange way it does, news of the fight flashed throughout the school and in the briefest of time the steps grew thronged with boys, all jostling each other and bellowing at the tops of their voices: and it encouraged Nathan no end to hear so many boys were for him.

'Go on, new boy!' they roared. 'Take Pennington down a notch or two.'

Then, when it seemed that the fighting and shouting had been going on for hours and not the few minutes it actually had been, another voice, raised, yet neither ranting nor angry, cut through the great hullabaloo.

'Worthwhile poetry,' it said, 'will never be composed while you insist on committing murder in so noisy a fashion. Can't you wretched little slugs at least kill each other quietly?' And Lavender, smartly dressed in a blue silk dressing-gown, swept down to pull Pennington and Nathan apart, disdainfully holding them at arm's length from each other like two naughty puppies. This was just as well for Nathan had begun to tire, yet it cheered him to see the smudge of blood under Pennington's nose.

'O-h, Lavender,' wailed the other boys, disappointed to lose their sport.

'Bloodthirsty little savages,' said Lavender, shoving Pennington away. In passing, Pennington shot Nathan the blackest of looks before pushing through the crowds and stomping down the stairs.

'It was a fair fight, Lavender,' complained the boys, who did not notice Pennington pinch and pull hair whenever he was able. 'You should have left 'em to it.'

> 'Peace hath her victories
> No less renowned than war . . . '

quoted Lavender, knowing nothing disperses a bad-tempered crowd of Moonville boys quicker than poetry (particularly his own, which had cleared a rugby match before now, sending players and spectators fleeing as if for their lives). It worked just as well this time. With heavy groans the boys drifted away, and Lavender smiling wistfully at the power of words finally released his grip on Nathan's arm.

'Are you hurt?' he enquired.

Nathan brushed himself down in a way clearly meant to show he wasn't.

'Your trunk?' asked Lavender, nodding across at it.

Nathan straightened up. 'Yes, it's mine,' he said, sounding more sullen than he'd intended.

'Come on, I'll lend you a hand getting it upstairs.'

'*Thanks*, Lavender,' said Richie, aware of the great honour being done to them (and the lifting was certainly a lot easier!)

As they climbed up into it, Nathan discovered that the attic of the old house had been divided into a warren of tiny sleeping quarters, with three or four iron beds crammed into each. Richie already shared his room with Ducksfoot and his piglet, who slept on her very own bed.

'And Molly doesn't snore half so loudly as Ducksfoot either,' said Richie.

He lit a candle while Nathan and Lavender set the trunk at the foot of the fourth, unclaimed, bed.

'Oh,' said Nathan, needlessly patting his pockets. 'I've just remembered, I don't have the key.'

Richie plonked himself down on the mattress, swinging his feet. 'You don't need one,' he remarked casually. 'Fulbert broke the lock. I must say, your cook at home packed you a delicious fruit cake.'

'You've eaten it?' said Nathan surprised.

'Of course, it's the rule. We always eat a new boy's grub in case none of us likes him and he turns out to be as insufferable as Pennington.'

'Ah yes, Pennington,' said Lavender frowning. 'A word of warning, Hilliam, you have made yourself a dangerous enemy there. Pennington is a particularly nasty bully.'

'Perhaps Sam should learn poetry to defend himself,' said Richie, bouncing up and down on the bed at his own cleverness.

Lavender grimaced. 'I shall let that remark pass,' he said.

With his back to the other two, Nathan lifted the lid of Sam's trunk curious to discover what was now his and a small whistle of delight escaped him when he saw. Was it possible, he wondered, that so many clothes were meant for one person—for him in fact—and every item so carefully washed and folded.

Upon the clothes lay a covering of fine cake crumbs, and tucked away in a corner Nathan noticed a solemn little black book. He picked it up and read aloud its title, '*A Comprehensive Guide to Etiquette—Most Suitable for a Young Gentleman.*' Attached to it was a note from Mr Smeasle urging, *Use it well.*

Being Mr Smeasle, of course, the book was not new and its cover hung by a thread. Nathan handed the book to Richie, who after mopping up the last few remaining crumbs with his finger casually tossed it into a corner where it stayed.

'Here, Hilliam, I suggest you put this on,' said Lavender, pulling a neatly laundered nightshirt from the trunk and throwing it at Nathan. 'You haven't stopped yawning for the past five minutes.'

'Heavens, Lavender, you must be joking,' exclaimed Richie. 'It's far too early for bed—why it's hardly dark at all and I haven't even shown Sam the woods yet.'

'The woods? He'd fall asleep before you reached halfway,' said Lavender. 'Isn't that so, Hilliam?'

'I do feel very tired,' admitted Nathan somewhat guiltily. 'I think Lavender may be right, Richie—at least for tonight.' He took off his jacket and hung it over the bed post.

'Come on, Tadcaster,' said Lavender. 'Leave your friend to his dreams. There is plenty of time for him to get used to our ways of doing things.'

Richie shrugged. 'Goodnight, Sam,' he said at the doorway. 'I'll show you the woods tomorrow if you like.'

Nathan smiled sleepily. 'Yes, I'd like that. G' night.'

He blew out the candle and finished undressing by starlight. Climbing into bed, his eyes flickered once, twice, then he fell deeply asleep.

Nathan's eyes opened suddenly. It was much later and darker. He lay still, certain that a loud sound and bright light had roused him from his sleep. He blinked through the darkness and seeing three empty beds remembered where he was.

'Moonville,' he murmured, its very name soft and oddly reassuring. It made him feel drowsy and his eyes began to close.

Before they had done so completely the loud crackling sound returned, arising from somewhere high up in the air. Leaping from bed, Nathan reached the tiny cobwebby window just in time to catch a spectacular burst of blue and green light amongst the stars, growing, fading, then shooting out fronds of silvery gold, which dropped to earth as fiery red dust.

When the last twinkle disappeared, Nathan remained kneeling on the window-ledge, head cocked and listening—but this time he was listening to something very much closer.

' . . . I tell you he's in with Tadcaster and Ducksfoot,' said the voice (from outside in the corridor). 'That oaf Lavender even helped with his trunk.'

Even whispered, the voice betrayed its speaker. It was Pennington, and Nathan guessed who he was looking for and why.

EIGHT

Nathan shook his head, quickly ridding it of the last stale crumbs of sleep. He was thinking more clearly now. Nimbly he crossed the floor, snatching up a heavy bolster on the way, and took up a position behind the open doorway.

Outside, in the corridor, Budd and Snookingworth, who made up Pennington's gang, were not being at all co-operative.

'No, you pay us the sixpence *now*,' Nathan heard a voice hiss (it was Snookingworth's).

'That's sixpence each,' put in a second voice (Budd).

'Oh, very well,' said Pennington peevishly. 'But I consider it a slight on my honour that you demand payment first.'

'Blow your honour,' said Budd, 'just give us our sixpences.'

Nathan heard the muffled jangle of coins in a pocket.

Pennington said, 'There, you have it, a shilling between you, I trust I have bought your services at last?'

'Hmm. And what exactly do we do for our money?' asked Budd, pacified.

'Rough up the new boy,' said Pennington spitefully. 'First, bundle him up in his blankets so I can lay on him a punch or two—'

'And of course the new boy'll be unable to strike you back,' said Snookingworth sarcastically.

'Then,' continued Pennington, ignoring him, 'then we'll toss him in the blankets until he feels so sick he begs us to stop.'

'And do we?'

'Perhaps—but only to hang him from the window by his heels.'

Standing perfectly still against the wall, Nathan heard Pennington list out his planned tortures for him and half raised the bolster in readiness.

'Come on,' whispered Pennington to his gang. 'Be sure not to wake him until the very moment we all pounce on him together.'

Not unless I pounce on you first, thought Nathan, his heart beginning to thump in anticipation. He saw the darkness stir as a figure crept into the room and immediately swung the bolster at it, giving Pennington a surprise hit in the face and causing him to fall back in a tangle with Budd and Snookingworth. In fact the blow was so hard that the bolster burst open and a dramatic feather blizzard added even more confusion to the scene, along with Snookingworth's shouts and Budd's roars. Pennington opened his mouth to join in with them, but instead swallowed a feather and began to cough and retch. Nathan trod on him as he fled the room, out into the darkened corridor—feathers spinning in his wake.

Of course he had no idea where was best to run—the roof of the house was a complete rookery of tiny, crooked rooms, crammed with beds and trunks; and more beds spilt out into the corridor. But by bouncing from one bed to the next, Nathan speedily made his way along it.

And as he flew between mattresses he heard Pennington and his gang give chase. In mid air, with his freshly washed nightshirt billowing about him, Nathan must have been as clear to them as a waving flag.

Then worse—suddenly the corridor ended. Like a swimmer treading water, Nathan bounced up and down on the last bed, staring at a door in a wall. On the door a sign read—

'NO BOY BEYOND THIS POINT—
BY ORDER OF B. BENTBEEF'

'He *must* stand and fight now!' whooped Snookingworth close behind.

It did appear that way, even to Nathan, for when he jumped down off the bed and tried the door, it was locked. He panicked, feeling himself cornered like one of Jago's vermin.

Yet the door had to have another side. Nathan hammered on it with his fists until the old door shook in its frame. More desperately he put his shoulder to it. To his surprise he heard a splintering sound and the lock and door parted company and the door hung crookedly open, revealing another long stretch of dark, windowless corridor (but one quite empty of beds). Without thinking where it might lead, Nathan took off down it.

'Damn his luck!' swore Pennington. 'But we'll get him yet.'

'I'm beginning to think this worth more than your meagre sixpence, Pennington,' said Budd in a sly, calculating way.

'Get Hilliam and I'll double it!'

A whole shilling more! thought Nathan on hearing this. He'll need to do better than that if he wishes to catch me. He sprinted down the empty corridor, his feet beating upon naked boards, while cobweb-shrouded doors flashed by on either side. When he saw that the passage ended at a blank wall, he turned to the nearest side-door. It wasn't locked, but once inside there was no way to secure it either. He looked around. An ancient four-poster bed without curtains and a small dormer window. Unfortunately the window was nailed so tightly to its frame that it wouldn't so much as rattle. Short of smashing the glass it offered no way out at all.

That left the bed. Nathan glanced at its canopy. At least it would give him the advantage of height and that was better than nothing. Quickly he shinned up one of the bulbous columns and, as he lay panting in the thick dust on top, Pennington, Snookingworth, and Budd skidded into the room. Pale starlight angled through the dirty window, and by it Nathan saw Pennington look up at him and grin.

'Well, well, Hilliam, where is Lavender to protect you now, I wonder?' he said in a nasty, teasing voice. 'Writing his sonnets, no doubt, and rhyming his words—far too busy to come and save your neck *this* time.'

Nathan was furious. 'At least *I* don't have to hire him to fight my battles, Pennington, or come sneaking up in the dark like a coward.' Then he smiled, remembering. 'Oh, and I hope the taste of feathers was to your liking.'

An ugly scowl appeared on Pennington's face. 'Bring him down!' he ordered.

Neither Snookingworth nor Budd was as light-footed as Nathan, and their assault on the old bed made it sway and creak. Pennington immediately saw his chance of lengthening Nathan's torment, and calling his cronies down ordered them to stand at opposite columns and shake the bed until it fell to pieces.

'Let's give Hilliam a rough ride before we knock him out of his tree.'

Eager for their extra shilling, Snookingworth and Budd shook and shook until every wooden joint was worked loose. The creaking canopy swung like a mad pendulum and the air grew so hazy with dust that every breath tasted of it.

Nathan, who refused to beg them to stop, clung on as best he could, his teeth rattling in his head.

It was then that he caught sight of the figure in the doorway. Something caught his eye making him look up and there he was. A small, cross man in a quilted smoking-jacket done up with string, and on his head a cap set slightly to one side, its tassel almost threadless. He was frowning as he watched the frenzied attack on the bed.

'P-Pennington, stop!' called Nathan, trying to warn him.

'Stop?' said Pennington. 'Why, this is hardly started. This is just to warm you up a little—'

His taunt went unfinished because, unseen behind his back, the man had reached into the pocket of his smoking-jacket, taken something out, and dashed it to the floor. The result was a blinding flash of white light.

When next Nathan was able to peer down, Pennington, Budd, and Snookingworth had vanished and could be heard thundering back up the corridor like scalded cats.

Nathan and the man gazed at each other in mutual interest.

'It is perfectly safe now,' said the man softly, almost in a whisper. 'You may climb down if you so wish.' He carefully cleared his throat. 'My name, should you care to know it, is Mr Gentleman.'

NINE

Because Mr Gentleman spoke so softly and had such an amicable manner, Nathan didn't feel at all afraid of going down and standing before him. The air smelt strongly of gunpowder, with wisps of smoke lingering here and there. Upon the floor sparkled tiny splinters of glass, which Nathan was careful to avoid in his bare feet.

'W-what was that?'

Mr Gentleman smiled shyly and dug into his pocket a second time, taking out and holding up something that resembled a large glass marble.

'I call it a lightning bomb,' he said. 'I invented it to surprise villains—although I suppose it does just as well against bullies.'

He held it out to Nathan, who drew back a little.

'Don't worry,' said Mr Gentleman, 'it won't harm you. You have to throw it very hard to break the glass, and that is the only way to make a flash.'

With extreme care Nathan took it from him and examined it more closely. 'Well it certainly gave Pennington a good shake,' he said laughing.

When he had finished turning it this way and that, Mr Gentleman took the lightning bomb from him and popped it back into his pocket. Nathan stroked his arms and shivered.

'Ah, but how thoughtless of me—you are cold,' said Mr Gentleman. 'Please, follow me.'

Before Nathan could ask him where, Mr Gentleman went out into the corridor and Nathan followed him into another small room, empty but for a fireplace. However, there was no fire burning in its grate to warm himself by, and Nathan saw that the blackened hearthstone stood out at a curious angle. With a sudden tingle of excitement he realized that this was because it was the uncovered entrance to a flight of steps.

Mr Gentleman started down them at once, until only his face showed. 'Now,' he said mysteriously, 'come through to my home.'

Nathan descended after him, the stairs corkscrewing tightly beneath his feet and his head full of questions. 'But . . . but, sir, who are you?' he suddenly burst out.

Mr Gentleman didn't reply and Nathan heard him chuckle. Then, before he knew it, he was stepping out past a drawn curtain into a vast circular room shaped like the inside of a drum.

'Welcome to my tower,' said Mr Gentleman holding out his arms in greeting. 'I say *my* tower, though by rights I am the master of all Moonville.'

'But the school and Mr Bentbeef—' began Nathan.

'Mr Bentbeef, when he remembers to pay, rents the rest of the house from me. I have no need of it and Mr Bentbeef's school prevents it from getting ruinously damp and over-run by mice, and generally falling into disrepair.'

Nathan wondered if this was so wise: mice couldn't carve their initials into old oaken panelling, or slide down bannisters or smash windows with catapults . . .

Mr Gentleman touched him gently on the shoulder, making these thoughts suddenly vanish. 'Please be good enough to turn that wheel beside you,' he said. 'It will move the hearth back into position. You see, I much prefer to keep myself apart from the day to day world.'

Nathan did as he was asked, hearing a distant grinding sound at the top of the stairway; then he lifted his head to take a full and proper look at the room before him.

He saw first that he was completely surrounded by books—shelves and shelves of them, rising in four galleries to the vaulted roof, so that several funny little ladders on wheels were required to reach the topmost ones. Great hefty tomes also lay scattered about on tables, or were piled up on the floor, with special pages marked with snippets of paper, envelopes, pipe-cleaners, and even a sock or two. A grand fireplace with a coat of arms carved on its sloping marble mantel housed a leaping log fire and this, along with many clusters of candles, gave the only light, since the windows were too narrow to let in anything more than a dusting of starlight: and still all the candles and burning logs combined were hardly enough even to catch the gold-leaf on the spines of the multitude of books.

Above, from the darkened ceiling, hung heraldic flags as thick as carpets, and beneath them suits of armour did for coat-stands. Among so many impressive things only the *most* impressive managed to stand out in any way—a brass telescope here, a globe there, an orrery in a dusty corner; and set further back on shelves were bottles such as would be found in an apothecary's shop, each containing a bright, translucent liquid and the small, slightly wizened body of a pickled animal or fish.

The room was a cross between a medieval castle and a laboratory, and was also Mr Gentleman's home—though clearly he put no great stress on either comfort or housekeeping. A couch was good enough for his bed and dirty plates and clothes lay wherever Nathan turned; but it was to the jars of preserved creatures that his eyes kept returning.

'Mr Gentleman,' he said in an awed whisper. 'What is it that you do here in your tower?'

Mr Gentleman looked at him, amused. 'Well, I'm not a wizard practising the black arts, if that's what you fear. No . . . no, I firmly believe in the possibilities of science, not magic. Would you care for some tea?'

Nathan nodded automatically and Mr Gentleman sat down on an old chair beside the fire and indicated that

Nathan should move aside a pile of books and sit on the chair facing him, on the opposite side.

Perhaps he is absent-minded and has already forgotten about the tea, thought Nathan, too polite to mention it. Yet presently he heard a puffing sound, and looking back around his chair was surprised to see a kettle on wheels approach him down a set of rails—quite like a little train. Before it, the kettle pushed a teapot (also on wheels) and behind came several wagons of cups, saucers, and spoons, with a jug of milk and a bowl of sugar. The kettle was raised up on a small alcohol burner, and as the water grew hotter so the train of tea things built up more and more speed, until every piece of china was rattling. The water was boiling violently when the train finally hit a set of buffers close to Nathan's feet, whereupon the kettle tipped up on a spring and emptied itself into the waiting teapot—and so tea was served!

Nathan laughed aloud and clapped his hands in appreciation.

'A mere toy,' said Mr Gentleman modestly. 'But it will not work so well for cocoa—the milk keeps boiling over and derailing the wagons.'

They drank their tea in silence, until Mr Gentleman said, 'Why do you keep staring up at my books?'

His question flustered Nathan. 'Oh, I did not mean to be rude, sir, it's just seeing so many books together . . . '

'Surely you have books in Mr Bentbeef's school. It has a library, does it not?'

'It has an empty room *called* a library,' answered Nathan. 'Richie Tadcaster—he's my friend—told me he once found a stray sheep inside it.'

Mr Gentleman's eyebrows arched. 'Indeed—what kind of school is this that Mr Bentbeef keeps under my roof?'

'I don't think a very good one, sir. All the boys ever do all day is gamble.'

'Gamble?'

'Yes, sir. On frogs mostly. But if a boy spots two flies on Duckfoot's pig, he's sure to make a wager on which of the flies will be first to reach the pig's ear. Oh, the pig is part of the school too, sir. Her name is Molly.'

'As good a name for a pig as any other, I shouldn't wonder,' observed Mr Gentleman chuckling. 'But you would rather *there were* books in this school of yours?'

Nathan nodded eagerly. 'Yes, sir. The more the better. If I were allowed to read I wouldn't mind about anything else.'

As he spoke, a chiming clock came alive with a procession of skeletons and angels, and among them too a Father Times, a smiling sun, and a sleeping moon in a bed cap. Mr Gentleman jumped up and checked the hour against his pocket watch.

'Midnight,' he said with satisfaction.

'Do you have an appointment?' asked Nathan.

'An appointment? Yes, of sorts,' replied Mr Gentleman smiling to himself. 'If you wish, you may accompany me.'

'In my nightshirt!' exclaimed Nathan.

'It isn't far. Here, take this coat, it'll keep the worst of the night's chill off you.'

Mr Gentleman took the cup and saucer from Nathan's hand and gave him a coat whose collar was silky beaver fur. Nathan slipped it on and followed Mr Gentleman up through the shelves of books until the ceiling and the stiff banners were near enough to touch. Down below, Nathan saw the fire glowing distantly as if at the bottom of a deep pit. Then Mr Gentleman started up a short ladder and passing through a trapdoor, led Nathan out on to the tower's flat roof. Nathan shivered as he stepped out on to the cold lead; his feet were bare and extremely dirty by now.

'The view up here is particularly fine,' remarked Mr Gentleman.

It was indeed. From the parapet Nathan gazed down on the dark woodlands behind the school, and further off lay the grey, rolling Downs. But the tower seemed to look more towards the sky than the land, and it thrilled Nathan to see the many stars. They appeared like countless microscopic shrimps at the bottom of a vast, inky ocean— the tiniest ones half-imagined twinkles, the larger ones magically surrounded by haloes of blue or green, which changed colour or vanished as quickly as soap bubbles.

Mr Gentleman watched him and said, 'Do you know what they call a man who spends his nights gazing up at the stars?'

Nathan immediately pictured Jago fallen into the gutter. 'A drunkard, sir?'

Mr Gentleman tittered with amusement. 'A drunkard . . . very good. Very good indeed . . . ha-ha.' And Nathan blushed, knowing he had said something foolish. 'Well, yes, that is the first kind,' agreed Mr Gentleman. 'I am the second kind. An astronomer.'

'*Astronomer?*'

Mr Gentleman nodded. 'Surely you have heard that the Gentleman family is noted for astronomy? My grandfather, Sir Humphrey Gentleman, had this very tower built especially to launch his balloon, which he used to study the rings of Saturn. There is a rather fine portrait of him in the Great Hall.'

Nathan remembered the angry-faced man with a fork sticking from the end of his nose, and quickly moved the subject on.

'You mentioned an appointment, sir,' he said.

'Ah, yes.' Mr Gentleman stooped to light a lantern and soon its yellow glow fanned out across the entire roof.

'But aren't those fireworks?' said Nathan, seeing an impressively large rack of them set up nearby. 'Was it you who set them off before?'

'Not fireworks,' corrected Mr Gentleman firmly. 'Fireworks are for small boys and Chinese mandarins. These are rockets. And yes, it was me before. A rocket at ten o'clock, two at eleven o'clock, and three now it is midnight.'

'But why?' asked Nathan.

Mr Gentleman's reply was both simple and mysterious. 'It's my way of talking to the stars,' he said.

For the moment he added no more but stepped forward to light a single fuse which linked the trio of rockets together. It began to fizzle and Mr Gentleman hurried back to join Nathan, standing a safe distance away. As they waited, there came an angry rush of flame and the first rocket streaked high into the sky, exploding into a mass of blue stars and silver beams; soon after, the second rocket followed and was a sparkling green cascade of firecrackers; then it was the turn of the third rocket, which shot out twenty golden comets, each with its own long red tail.

'Have you finished talking to the stars now?' whispered Nathan in the smoky silence that followed.

'For the time being,' answered Mr Gentleman contentedly.

'And . . . and do the stars ever talk back to you?'

Mr Gentleman smiled but did not reply.

Nathan shook his head. 'I don't really understand this at all well, sir,' he admitted.

Mr Gentleman led him back to the trapdoor. 'Really it is quite easy,' he said in a brisk, rather matter-of-fact way that Nathan just knew would not be easy at all. Climbing down into the tower, Mr Gentleman said, 'I am a *planetarian*. That is, I strongly believe in the possibilities of other worlds peopled with intelligent beings like ourselves. The rockets are my way of making myself known to them. Do you think me odd?'

'I wouldn't care to say, sir,' said Nathan. 'I've never met a planetarian before.'

He heard Mr Gentleman's familiar chuckle.

Together they went down through the tower. By the fire Nathan took off the borrowed coat and warmed himself before the flames.

'I must go soon,' he said.

Mr Gentleman rose up and solemnly extended his hand. 'Pleased to have met you . . . '

'Sam,' said Nathan quickly. 'Sam Hilliam, and thank *you*, sir, it's been most entertaining.' They shook hands as friends.

'Well, Sam, before you leave I insist you borrow a book from me. It seems only right, after all I have so many. Unlike Mr Bentbeef!'

'Can I?' said Nathan keenly. 'Do you really mean it?' He thought the offer over. 'After meeting my very first planetarian I think I should like to learn more about the stars.'

This pleased Mr Gentleman, who selected a book he thought suitable and gave it to Nathan, along with a candle to light his return journey through the secret passageway.

'I'll see that the broken door is mended in the morning,' said Mr Gentleman. 'Meanwhile, if you wish to visit me again there is a small door tucked away at the foot of the tower, although you may find the brambles before it a little fierce.'

'So I may visit you again?' asked Nathan.

'Of course, you must return my book—and borrow others if you care to.'

With this kind offer they parted company and Nathan, holding the candle before him, made his way back to the crowded dormitories. He kept a wary eye open for Pennington, but it was Richie he saw first, looking like a country gentleman with a gun thrown over his shoulder and a brace of pigeon in his hand. With him was Ducksfoot similarly dressed and armed, and Molly scurried about their feet like a gun-dog.

'Oh, *there* you are, Sam,' cried Richie on seeing him, and he stared at Nathan's hand. 'What on earth have you there?' he asked.

'A book,' said Nathan.

'Heavens,' said Richie at the sheer novelty.

TEN

After two weeks at Mr Bentbeef's establishment, Nathan at last acquired the typical tousled look of a Moonville boy, and there was a smudge of lasting grime on his face. This was not because the school lacked water (why, the stuff leaked through the roof after every storm) and Nathan had even heard rumours of a bath; but for a boy to wash himself in a bath would be considered shocking, since everyone agreed baths were for keeping frogs in. Besides, as Richie said, making yourself clean requires such effort, while staying dirty more or less takes care of itself.

Several more weeks later and Nathan's uniform no longer marked him out as *the new boy*. His knees were clean through his trousers and his jacket pockets hung as flaps—torn whilst climbing up the ivy to his bedroom window—or was it from the time he and Richie had built their treehouse over in the woods?

There was honour in shabbiness—except in the case of a scrawny, grey-skinned boy called Mungbone, whom Pennington took great delight in bullying. For some reason Mungbone attracted moths and his clothes were riddled with tiny, fraying holes, the moths flying up from him whenever he moved; and when he left a place there remained behind a faint, musty smell, like mould.

Apart from Pennington, life at Moonville was fairly free and easy. Left to their own devices, Nathan and Richie spent many nights roaming the woods together, both getting as grubby as possible. The school—or rather its grounds—came more alive during the night than at any hour of the day, the darkness giving the necessary cover to go hunting. For this purpose, many boys kept a fire-arm of some description, be it an ancient blunderbuss, or rusting musket, or a duelling pistol secretly slipped to them by a rakish uncle—only the farm boys owning anything halfway decent or modern; while the main requirement of this motley armoury was to shoot pigeon and rabbit, or occasionally a hare or duck.

This was not idle sport. Had the boys tried to survive on the rations doled out to them by Mr Bentbeef, his rancid bacon, tasteless porridge, and a particularly stomach-churning stew made from greasy slops, they would have starved. Some nights the sound of gunfire and smell of powder was so great it was as if the Battle of Waterloo was being fought. The wonder of it was no boy was shot!

Most days were torpid compared to the nights (unless cricket was played—cricket was an altogether different affair, more like Waterloo without the guns but with hand-to-hand combat instead). In class, however, Nathan was content enough to pass his time on a window-sill reading one of Mr Gentleman's books. Except for the occasional sarcastic word from Pennington, who would also try snatching his book away in a half-hearted manner that showed he was wary, Nathan was like the quiet centre of a storm. Around him flour bombs exploded, frogs raced, and ale was downed. In fact the boys were able to do whatever they liked, so long as Lavender was left free to put up his feet and compose his epic verse, or study form in the newspapers for the Newmarket races.

Yet he always made sure to post a look-out, ready to warn of Mr Bentbeef's approach so that, by the time the headmaster arrived, every boy was sitting in a row chanting his eight times table or the books of the Old Testament.

'Remember what I said about medicine and heddication, Lavender,' cooed Mr Bentbeef, hooking his thumbs beneath his gown. 'Are you making it sufficiently dry for these young heads?'

'Indeed, Mr Bentbeef,' Lavender assured him. 'As dry as the bread you served us last night for supper.'

'Splendid! Then carry on.'

' . . . eight eights are seventy-one, nine eights are eighty-six . . . ' chanted the class dutifully until Mr Bentbeef was safely away down the corridor and usual business could continue as before.

Then on one particular morning Mr Bentbeef came breathlessly through the door as if he had run all the way from his house. Ignoring Lavender, he said to Nathan, 'A word with you, Hilliam, if you please.' And when Nathan went forward he found Mr Bentbeef's arm about him and himself whisked out of the door.

Mr Bentbeef had an expectant glow about him. 'This arrived in the morning post for you, Hilliam. It's from your guardian, I . . . umm . . . could tell as much by the postmark, and I thought it may be important enough to need your immediate attention.'

He handed Nathan a badly re-sealed envelope and hung back, obviously waiting for him to open it.

Good old Sam, thought Nathan smiling to himself, he's kept his side of the bargain and written to Mr Smeasle for money. He desperately needed money, he already owed Richie seven shillings and sixpence. He opened the letter and read:

> *My Dear Ward,*
>
> *I read your letter outlining your present hardships and must confess to feelings of astonishment as all provision for your schooling has been fully met. I have, however, against all better judgement, decided to send you a bill to the value of five pounds to cover your present*

embarrassment. I warn you, this moment of weak generosity on my part will not be repeated this side of Christmas.

I hope you are in good health and study hard, etc.

Yr. ob. servant
R. J. Smeasle

P.S. Although you paint a glowing picture of yourself at your new school, I note that your spelling and punctuation remain as abysmal as ever!

Folded into the bottom of the letter was a five pound note.

Nathan looked up grinning, to find Mr Bentbeef hovering before him.

'Not bad news, I trust?' he enquired unconvincingly.

'Er, no, sir. A few lines from my guardian, Mr Smeasle, that's all.'

He edged back, meaning to return to his class, which was dully chanting nonsense under Lavender's supervision.

Mr Bentbeef pressed his podgy fingers together, peering over them with bright, focused eyes. 'While you are here, Hilliam,' he said, 'I must have words with you on a delicate business. I see by my accounts that your music fees remain unpaid.'

'But I don't do music, sir,' protested Nathan.

'Tish, Hilliam, all boys at Moonville do music. Such wonderful, lusty voices.'

In the background, as if to prove his point, someone hollered, 'Ow, Thistlewaite, stop twisting me ear!'

'A small matter of five pounds,' pressed Mr Bentbeef, stepping forward and breathing more heavily. 'I am sure you will wish to clear the debt as soon as possible.'

Nathan realized he was caught in a well laid trap.

Reluctantly his hand went out and he saw the five pound note, which had not been in his possession above two minutes, snatched away by Mr Bentbeef in one greedy pounce.

He licked his lips. 'Thank you, dear boy,' he said, and with a twirl of his dark gown was gone.

That night, in the tower, Nathan described to Mr Gentleman how he had been expertly fleeced by the headmaster.

'Five pounds!' he wailed, at the memory of his loss.

By now his visits to Mr Gentleman had become daily, and not only to select a new book to take away and devour. Sometimes he came to hear Mr Gentleman talk at length about the Universe. At other times, if Mr Gentleman was too busy to talk, Nathan was sure to find himself mixing powders, or copying out star-charts, or assembling a telescope. Just as often there were the simple chores to be seen to, like stirring up the dying fire, or watching over Mr Gentleman's supper of broth to stop it boiling away. Each visit was entirely different, and yet he never once mentioned them to anyone, not even Richie, for at school Mr Gentleman was considered so eccentric as to be a figure of fun.

Mr Gentleman, kneeling in front of the fire, was trying to toast bread on a fork, but for every slice that got buttered another would burst into flames.

'Mr Bentbeef behaves quite outrageously,' he said, frowning at yet another black, smoking failure. 'Perhaps you should write to your guardian and tell him.'

'Oh no,' said Nathan, horrified. 'I shouldn't like to trouble him over something so small. But five pounds! I wish that it were small to me.'

Mr Gentleman looked up at him, his eyes dark and intelligent in the firelight. 'Sam, I will give you five pounds,' he said, 'if you will agree to help me.'

Nathan bit into his toast and gazed back with interest.

'I too have received a letter,' explained Mr Gentleman. 'There is to be a meeting of my fellow planetarians up in Edinburgh. Normally I would refuse such an invitation because of the importance of setting off my rockets at their appropriate times. But now I believe I can travel to Scotland safe in the knowledge that I leave behind a person who will manage the task well enough without me.'

'Me?' cried Nathan. 'You are willing to pay me five pounds for that? Why, I would happily do it for nothing.'

'No,' said Mr Gentleman. 'I shall have more peace of mind if it is a business arrangement between us. Do you say yes to it?'

'Of course! Oh, look out, Mr Gentleman, your toast is on fire!'

Mr Gentleman carelessly threw down the toasting-fork and without another word crossed over to the bookshelves. There, making no attempt to hide what he did, he lifted the lid of a small tin box so that Nathan clearly saw the heap of banknotes inside it. The box was crammed so full that notes fell out and fluttered to the floor.

'Bother,' said Mr Gentleman, as if so much untidy money was a nuisance not a blessing.

He brought one of the notes back to Nathan and pushed it into his hand.

'Keep it safe from Mr Bentbeef,' he warned. 'I set off a week on Sunday.'

ELEVEN

On the Sunday morning in question, Nathan accompanied Mr Gentleman from his tower to the road where Mr Rabbitson's pony and trap waited to carry him to the station. In daylight, away from his dim tower, Mr Gentleman looked particularly small and pale, blinking at the bright light like a puzzled mole. Without him saying so, Nathan had the distinct impression that it had been a long time since he was last away from home, and on such a promising June day as this he was unsuitably dressed in a heavy overcoat.

Mr Rabbitson nodded shyly to Nathan and began the business of loading up the luggage. For the pony's sake it was a good job that most of the journey to the station was downhill. Apart from Nathan and the two men there was no one else in sight and behind them the school stood as silent as a ruin: at half-past nine most of its boys would still be in their beds, asleep.

Mr Gentleman caught Nathan's arm and drew him aside, pressing a large key into his hand. Nathan recognized it as the one that opened the small, awkward door at the base of the tower.

'Are you quite sure you want to give me this?' he asked.

Mr Gentleman nodded. 'I would worry if it were someone else,' he said. 'And, Sam, it may be that I'm away for a while longer than I told you. Sir Ecton Burrows, a fellow planetarian, has kindly invited me to his home in Yorkshire to view his new telescope.'

This was news to Nathan. 'How long will you be away?' he asked.

Mr Gentleman shook his head unknowingly, then he unclipped his pocket watch and held it out to Nathan.

'Take this too,' he said. 'The local church clock is not at all accurate and this only gains by a minute or two a week. Remember, Sam, it is important to set off the rockets exactly on time. You *know* why?'

'In case telescopes on other worlds watch us like we would watch them,' answered Nathan dutifully.

'Precisely, and the more regular the rockets are, the better. They might persuade our watching friends that we are intelligent beings and so answer us back.'

Nathan accepted the handsome time-piece, clasping it to the side of his head to hear the steady tick of its mechanical heart.

'Begging your pardon, Mr Gentleman,' said Mr Rabbitson giving an awkward cough.

'Very good, Mr Rabbitson, I am coming.'

'Safe journey,' wished Nathan, suddenly realizing that he would greatly miss his company.

Mr Gentleman climbed up beside Mr Rabbitson and made himself comfortable. He gave a small wave and smile, and, with a final glance back at Moonville, moved slowly away.

Nathan watched the trap trundle down the hill until no longer able to make out Mr Gentleman's tiny, hunched figure. Then he gazed down at his hand—at the key that lay across his palm. He clutched it tightly and turned from the road.

Hurrying back to school, Nathan felt he didn't own a care in the world; his feet were so light he could fly. He had Mr Gentleman's fine watch and the key to his tower, which meant he could come and go as he pleased. Nathan smiled; why, even the bright clear morning seemed for him alone, and without another soul to share it he whistled jauntily to himself as he swaggered around the corner.

Then he stopped and the whistle died the same instant. Perhaps it had been quite wrong of him not to take into account others. In front of him he saw a suspicious looking trail of potato peelings that led some distance from the kitchen steps to a clump of bushes. The fact that the trail was incomplete revealed that whatever it had been laid for had been lured along it already, hurrying on in the greedy hope of something tastier at the end.

Nathan followed the same trail, and as he neared the bushes he heard whispered voices along with the stifled complaints of an animal. He found some bare branches where he could peer unseen into the hiding place, and who did he immediately spy there?—Pennington, Snookingworth, and Budd.

All three were dressed in nightshirts, Pennington's was as white as when new; Budd's and Snookingworth's were grey and grubby. One of Budd's sleeves was completely torn off, and Snookingworth had a large dark stain down his front, evidence of an ancient nosebleed. They each wore boots that were untied; and there was a sense of haste about the scene. Snookingworth hovered holding a saucepan and Pennington gripped a kitchen knife. Beneath his arm a small creature was desperately trying to break free.

Nathan peered harder at it. 'Why, that's Ducksfoot's Molly,' he told himself, frowning; and looking again at the knife that Pennington carelessly waved before him, shuddered as he guessed its purpose.

As before, Pennington was having trouble with his gang. 'I can't do this *all* by myself,' he complained. 'You did promise you would help, you told me you would.'

'But it don't seem right somehow,' replied Snookingworth. 'That's not no ordinary pig—it's Molly.'

'Look, I'll give you sixpence more,' said Pennington, resorting to his usual bribery.

'At that price you can buy sausages up at the local farm,' said Budd unimpressed.

'Ah, but think of the look on Ducksfoot's face when he finds his precious piggy-wiggy missing.'

Snookingworth held the saucepan awkwardly. 'But to catch her blood, Pennington, it'll make my stomach churn. I shall be sick, I know it.'

'I won't!' said Pennington. 'I shall be imagining the taste of black-pudding. And *you* won't be so squeamish either when you smell it frying in a pan.'

Budd and Snookingworth shuffled their feet, unconvinced. Nathan, however, had heard enough.

'Pennington—you're a vile, evil vampire!' he shouted, bursting in on them, branches snapping all around.

The three boys were taken by complete surprise. In fact Pennington was so rattled that, before he could stop himself, he threw Molly straight into Nathan's arms.

'Thanks,' grinned Nathan. He turned and ran like Tom the Piper's son, the ungrateful piglet squirming against his chest. In a matter of seconds Pennington had collected his wits and ran roaring after him, desperate to restore some lost honour. Behind him followed Budd and Snookingworth, going just fast enough to prove themselves loyal, without the slightest intention of ever catching up with Molly and her rescuer.

Nathan made straight for the safety of Mr Gentleman's tower. 'Hold still,' he told Molly as he tried to cope with the madly wriggling piglet and the key to the door. The door opened, and Molly, slipping from Nathan's grasp, went bolting inside. Nathan was right behind, but once he had shut the door there was no light to see by. In the darkness he heard Molly go scurrying up the stone steps.

'Oh, Molly, you know me well enough,' wailed Nathan after her. 'I'm not like Pennington, I won't hurt you!'

He stumbled up the steps to the landing, where he knew from memory there were two doors, the first that led directly into the tower, the second that opened on to a small, windowless storeroom. It was from here—the storeroom—that there came the sounds of the piglet blundering blindly about, squealing in terror and self-pity.

Nathan felt his way to the door and entered the musty-smelling room. Still unable to see a thing he reached into his pocket for his matches. He lit one and, while the flame still flared, he caught sight of a single word branded into the side of a barrel.

'Gunpowder!'

He threw down the match and stamped on it hard. What an idiot he was—he might have blown himself to pieces, for there wasn't just a single barrel of gunpowder (used by Mr Gentleman in the making of his rockets) but at least half a dozen, stacked one on top of another. And during the match's brief life, he also glimpsed a great pile of logs and kindling wood, enough to last Mr Gentleman through the next winter, and a small determined pink creature (although no longer quite so pink as before) which, now it was dark again, made her escape through Nathan's legs.

Nathan sighed. There was nothing for it but to let Molly into the main part of Mr Gentleman's tower, that way at least he could see what he was doing, even if it meant the risk of Molly charging into things and breaking them.

He opened the door and felt the air stir as Molly rushed past him. Perhaps then she noticed the pickled creatures in their glass jars and wondered if the same fate awaited her, because she immediately took fright again and went squealing up the steps towards the roof of the tower.

'Molly—stop, you brainless porker!' cried Nathan exasperated. 'Can't you see I'm trying to help you?'

Once more he ran after her, knowing that she would be cornered at the top. Molly soon realized this too: when Nathan appeared on the uppermost landing she had turned to meet him, her little eyes sparkling with fight. Nathan dived, gripping the piglet by the rear. Molly, indignant, struggled like never before. Nathan managed to heave himself back up on to his feet, then completely lost balance and fell against the bookcase. To both his and Molly's amazement the bookcase burst open and together they went crashing through it—what outwardly seemed to be a section of solid shelving turned out to be a secret door, cunningly disguised with false book spines.

In falling through the doorway, Nathan found himself wound up in shrouds of filthy cobwebs, and before he could cry out, Molly had leapt free of his arms. Yet it was only half an escape. Thinking quickly, Nathan kicked the door to, to stop her fleeing from the room, then stood up muttering and brushing himself down.

Only when *he* was good and ready did he look up to see where he was, and then he quickly became curious, more so when he realized that the room had been unvisited for years. At its furthest end a small, dirty window gave just enough light to explore by, yet for all his searching it revealed none of the things a secret room should contain and which Nathan luridly imagined he would find there. Mostly it was filled with wooden crates containing nothing more interesting than household accounts and bundles of dull, dutiful letters from distant cousins or estate managers—with hardly anything less than a hundred years old.

Then, set further back in the gloom, Nathan caught sight of two huge cylindrical tanks, almost hidden behind a wall of crates and curtained with cobwebs. He squeezed himself closer and, with his nose practically pressed up against them, found a metal plate which he managed to clean with his cuff.

'*Balloon Gas*,' he read aloud.

He wondered why he was not more surprised to find it here. Then he remembered Sir Humphrey Gentleman who had built the tower. Hadn't he also owned a balloon from which he could observe Saturn?

Now this *was* more exciting than heaps of old papers and Nathan began to search for other things connected with Sir Humphrey's balloon. Never did he expect to come upon the balloon itself, but he did, in a long, lead box that ran the entire length of the room and which was half buried under rubbish. Inside the box, the balloon's silken skin was neatly folded away and appeared remarkably well preserved. A wicker basket, now full of broken books, must have been the passenger-carrier, for at its corners were thick leather straps with metal clips on the end.

As pleased as Nathan was to find the balloon complete, his next discovery was the equal of it. In a corner he stumbled against a lever almost as high as himself, and by careful exploring found it was attached to some heavy metal ratchets and cogs that in turn joined the walls, ceiling, and floor. Keen to know what this curious arrangement did, Nathan quickly fetched a can of oil and spent over an hour applying it to every part of the mechanism. At last, when he was certain he could make it move, he spat into his hands and gripped the lever, pulling it with all his strength.

To begin with the lever was stiff and the cogs and ratchets were stubbornly locked; and the parts that did not groan and creak, clanked and rattled. But bit by bit, as the oil seeped through, it grew increasingly easier for Nathan to work the lever back and forth.

Then he stopped and the grind of cogs stopped with him. He stared at the door and saw to his amazement that it had shrunk.

'Why no,' he cried, at last understanding. 'It hasn't

shrunk at all, but the floor has risen higher;' and overhead he noticed that the ceiling had begun to part.

He worked the lever hard then, the floor rising inch by inch, while the ceiling opened out as neat in its contrivance as a beetle's wing or a music box where the lid divides to allow a tiny dancing figure to appear.

When the floor finally reached roof level the lever refused to move any more, and over Nathan's head stretched nothing but clear, blue sky. This he saw was a perfect launching place for Sir Humphrey's balloon, and he wondered if even Mr Gentleman was aware that his tower contained such a marvel.

'I shall tell him as soon as he returns,' announced Nathan proudly. Then seeing himself closely watched he burst out laughing. 'Oh, Molly!' he said remembering the poor forgotten creature, now turned black with dirt.

TWELVE

With Molly joyfully reunited with Ducksfoot and Pennington shamed throughout the school (although he hotly denied ever intending to harm Molly) Nathan felt free to enjoy Mr Gentleman's tower and all the learned and interesting books it contained. He read late into the night, always making sure, of course, to fire off Mr Gentleman's rockets at their appointed hours. Strangely, he was never afraid to be in the tower by himself—even at midnight, with the shadows nibbling at the edges of his candle light, or the bats flickering about him up on the roof. For him the tower was always friendly and welcoming, and the brilliant shooting flashes of each rocket were something he looked forward to with anticipation.

However, one thing he had not taken into account was Richie's jealousy of these long absences.

'Where do you keep disappearing to?' he demanded one evening as they sat together beneath the trees, Richie fretfully chewing on a blade of grass and Nathan reading. 'I search everywhere for you, but you're never to be seen. Perhaps you are avoiding me, Sam Hilliam, and you promised to help me finish our tree house.'

'And I *will*,' protested Nathan, using his book to shield his guilty face.

Richie was unconvinced. 'You're turning into a regular dull fellow, Sam,' he said. 'If you think more of me than your silly books you will prove it.'

'How?' asked Nathan.

'Easy—by spending the day with me at the seaside—we'll go this coming Saturday.'

'Beefy would never agree to it,' said Nathan, at last setting aside his book.

'Wouldn't he? Not even if we led him to believe we were going to Krundal to study the abbey ruins? That's the sort of dry, worthy thing that headmasters approve of. Besides,' he added airily, 'I don't think Beefy'd object too much to us going anywhere if it meant two less mouths to feed.'

And he was proved absolutely right. This was how Nathan found himself on the road to Sidpool, with Richie prattling excitedly beside him. The journey had meant a dawn walk to the village where a wagoner they were friendly with gave them a lift to Cudbury, and from there it was a further three miles on foot along a dusty road to Sidpool.

Nathan had never been to the coast before and now he found himself excitedly looking out for the sea at every bend in the road. The morning was very hot, but a gusty dry wind blew into his face making his eyes water. He rubbed them on the back of his hand and when he next looked up he saw a hazy patch of slate-green water.

'There it is! There it is!' he cried, running forward for a clearer view.

'Hey, wait for me!' wailed Richie.

Before its final descent into Sidpool, the road rose up giving an uninterrupted view of both the town and sea. Nathan stood by Richie, silently watching the wind-blown waves come tumbling in, flecking the air with foam. And along the promenade, behind the neat respectable boarding-houses, sheets cracked and flapped on washing-lines as if the very waves had been caught, skinned and hung out to dry.

'Race you there!' shouted Richie impetuously; and the two boys sprinted all the way down into the town, arriving breathless on the beach, where not a moment was wasted that could be mindlessly filled by digging holes, dodging waves or paddling with their trousers rolled up to their knees. After that there was a whole pier to explore, with swing-boats, gypsy fortune-tellers, a Punch and Judy show, and candyfloss stalls, all the way along to a paddle-steamer at the end. Then back to the beach where Richie made himself a sun-hat from his handkerchief against the afternoon glare, and Nathan decided that the twenty minute gap since the last time they had eaten was far too long and set off in search of toffee-apples.

Passing the donkey rides, he climbed the steps of the sea-wall onto the promenade, where invalids were lined up in bath-chairs, taking the air, and crowds swept by, noisy and smiling. Suddenly Nathan's idle steps came to an abrupt stop. Through the bright, milling throng, glaring at him in that angry, unflinching way Nathan remembered so well, loomed Jago Blint. Beside him was Nip half sitting across his master's boot, staring at Nathan in the same intense fashion. As ever, Jago wore his hat fringed with dead mice, in the heat attracting dozens of flies which fiercely buzzed around him and crawled across his unnervingly still face.

Instinctively Nathan turned and fled. He fought his way along the promenade until he saw a larger gathering of people and sought safety by diving in amongst it. A hand seized his collar and hauled him up like a fish on a line. ''Ere-'ere. You pays your penny, like everyone else,' demanded a dumpy woman angrily.

Without thinking, Nathan pulled out a coin and dropped it into her grubby palm. This put the woman into a better humour. 'That's the way, dearie. Now go stand over there behind the rope with the other paid folk—me guided tour will begin anon.'

Only then did Nathan realize that he had paid to see a travelling waxworks exhibition, housed in a shabby tent that no amount of flags and bunting could brighten. Yet he had no intention of waiting for a tour of its dubious attractions, and when the woman turned away he slipped through a raised flap that served for a door.

He narrowly missed bumping into Henry VIII.

Nathan halted before the figure, half in surprise, half in interest. Henry stood pot-bellied with his hands on his hips and his six rather jolly wives lined up next to him as if he were the keeper of a harem. Jane Seymour had a cracked foot which meant she leaned heavily against Anne Boleyn; and all the wives were alike with very red cheeks and gowns made of cheap material, trimmed to make it appear expensive; while much of their jewellery had missing stones. In one such gap (in Henry's chain of office) was a beer-bottle top on which was cheekily proclaimed 'Best Stout'.

This section was called 'Glorious Kings and Queens of England' and here keeping Henry and his wives company were William the Conqueror, Richard the Lionheart and his bad brother—John, Elizabeth, Charles II, and the severed head of Charles I. This was set on a table and surrounded with potted ferns like a pig's head served at a banquet.

Hurrying on, Nathan came to the next section, the sign above positively shrieking at him in large letters that spelt out 'Freaks'. And there, fashioned in wax, were assembled mermen and dog-faced children and a woman with a hand growing from her stomach and another with two heads facing different directions. This, Nathan found even more unsettling, swiftly passing under a third sign that read 'Fearful Criminals'.

The corner of the tent he now found himself in was deliberately much darker for dramatic effect and the trapped heat so intense that a bead of sweat trickled down the side of Nathan's head. Through the gloom he saw the gleam of glass eyes—murderous eyes— belonging to the likes of Sweeney Todd, Dick Turpin,

Spring-Heeled Jack, Jonathan Wild, and those notorious grave-robbers, Burke and Hare. Sweeney Todd, the Demon Barber, clutched a bloody cut-throat razor and grinned wickedly like he did in all the 'penny dreadfuls'; and an unhappy skeleton lay slumped at the feet of the grave-robbers, dimly lit by a lantern held in one of the robbers' hands.

The sea-wind made the roof and walls billow, and the shadows shifted back and forth creating the illusion of movement. Nathan stood staring, not daring to move, for to do so meant turning his back on one of these monsters. And yet, when a hand stole out, slowly . . . slowly, then grabbed him with a grip like death, it was almost as if he expected it would. Still the shock of it drained every bit of colour from his face. Remembering too late to struggle, he half turned to face the villain who had seized him. Of course it was none of the waxwork horrors. It was an altogether more different villain. It was Jago, his detested uncle.

'You come to view the wicked men o' the past, 'ast 'ee, Nattie?' he breathed, his face sweating in the heat-thickened air. 'Been quite a while, boy, ain't it, since me and you stood together like this? Perhaps you thought never to see the day again.'

A little way off the tour was just beginning. 'This 'ere be 'Enry the Eighth, ladies and gentlemen,' rose the voice of the dumpy woman. 'See 'im in all 'is pomp and glory. A monarch more gl-orious 'n' pompous than any uvver.'

Nathan felt reassured knowing that people were now within hearing distance. 'I'm not going back with you, Uncle,' he said with quiet defiance.

'Not coming home, Nattie? 'Course you are. We've a licence from King Charles to honour. His statue next door'll come alive and chase you if you don't.' His voice took on a menacing purr which made Nip cower. 'I

85

know all about you, Nathan Wheatear, and your grand pretence up at *that school*, acting so hoity-toity as I almosts tips me topper at you. But the next moment I sees clean through you, Nattie, to what you really are and shall always be.'

'. . . and this un 'ad 'er 'ead chopped oft, as did that un, and this un died of a broken 'eart for 'er dear 'Enery . . . ' continued the guide, sweeping her way along the row of Henry's wives.

'Please, Uncle, don't make me go with you,' pleaded Nathan. 'Let me stay at Moonville for a little longer. Please. Just a little longer.' He couldn't bear the thought of simply deserting his friends—especially Mr Gentleman who trusted him so completely.

To his surprise Nathan saw a smile appear on his uncle's face, a smile that was both sly and cunning. 'Why, Nattie, me fine boy, ain't I a man of great heart? In fact I don't believe no man has a greater heart than your Uncle Jago. I ain't in no big hurry to give away your secrets to your new-made friends, your new-made *rich* friends. And I *do* imagine thems are rich, Nat, and like most rich folk they tend to be more careless with what they have in plentiful supply. I'm sure a few of these *rich boys* wouldn't mind you helping out your Uncle Jago, who now finds himself skint on account of his expensive pursuit of an *ungrateful* nephew. Am I beginning to make meself crystal, Nat?'

Nathan understood perfectly. 'You want me to steal for you up at the school,' he said sourly.

'Steal, Nattie, steal? Now who mentioned such a thing? Steal is what villains do—villains like our present company. And they're justly hung from the gallows for it. But you can't steal from friends, Nattie boy, you merely borrow, then . . . sometimes . . . you forgets to pay back.'

Nathan felt so sick with rage and disgust that he

did not notice Jago's skilful fingers riffle through his pockets until they triumphantly drew out Mr Gentleman's watch; before thrusting it into his own pocket Jago dangled it in front of Nathan's face.

'I imagine pretty pieces like this are quite regular at that fine school of yorn.'

'But you can't!' cried Nathan as Jago snatched the watch away.

'Can't? Can't?' answered Jago pretending to be perplexed. 'Mightn't your uncle *borrow* like you must have done, Nat, for how else could you have come upon such a neat chimer, with its chain solid gold an' all? Remember, Nattie,' he grinned, prodding Nathan with a hard finger. 'I shall be watching and waiting for you— especially when you least expects it.'

With that he slowly took out a cigarette and lit it from the grave-robbers' lantern. Then, lazily straightening his hat, he strolled casually away blowing out smoke; only Nip at his heels bothering to look back.

Once more out in the hot sunshine, Nathan felt cold and shivery. He quickly found Richie.

'Sam, what is it?' cried Richie, glancing up and seeing him. 'You look perfectly dreadful.'

'I want to go back. *Now*. To Moonville,' said Nathan curtly.

'It was those oysters, wasn't it?' said Richie shaking his head. 'Lor', I knew we shouldn't have scoffed so many.'

THIRTEEN

Travelling slowly back to Moonville with their wagoner friend, Nathan was in no mind to talk, and as the wagon rumbled on through the dusty heat of late afternoon he sat apart in the back, lost in gloomy thoughts. As if haunted by a ghost he was unable to rid himself of Jago's sneering face, or shake off the sound of his voice; and as for his uncle's words, these remained so clear that they might have hovered shining in the air before him.

On reaching Moonville, Nathan had become so downcast that at the first opportunity he slipped away from Richie and entered the comforting silence of the tower. There he simply sat for a long while, glancing up only when the clock's chimes distracted him.

It was almost too dark to see when he finally forced himself to cross to the bookshelves. Before him a tin box gleamed dully, slyly tempting him. Slowly Nathan lifted its lid and a careless tangle of banknotes immediately sprang up until ready to spill out. How easy it would be to stuff a hundred pounds into his pocket and nobody— certainly not Mr Gentleman—would be any the wiser.

'No!'

His voice echoed eerily and his hand rested on the slammed lid. How could he think to take a single penny from Mr Gentleman? Wasn't it enough that he had allowed Jago to steal his watch?

At midnight Nathan dutifully fired off three rockets without bothering to glance up at them. But, as preoccupied as he was, one thought stayed perfectly clear—so long as he must be a thief he would not rob his friends of anything.

He left the tower soon after, and with just a candle to light his way climbed up Moonville's great sweeping stairway until it grew rickety and led only to the dead-end of the dormitories. Beneath the roof the day's heat lay trapped and stifling, convincing Nathan he was quite alone: the other boys unlikely to return until the cool of early morning.

He held up his candle.

A rookery of tiny rooms lay revealed before him and open to the corridor, their doors having been 'kidnapped' long ago, half as a prank and half in hope of gaining ransom. When the ransoms were unforthcoming the doors had been burned as firewood the next time it turned cold and Mr Bentbeef was slow and ungenerous with the coal. However, the room to which Nathan now crept had somehow managed to keep its door. On it, crudely carved, were the words 'Private. No admittance'.

This was Pennington's room. He shared it with Mungbone, the boy plagued by moths, and who Pennington treated no better than a pet slave. As a result, Pennington's was the neatest room in the entire school. Nathan pushed open the door and stood in the doorway, frowning as he gazed around. Pennington's clothes lay set out in scrupulous order, his night things together, his next clean shirt, set of underclothes, and socks together—everything rigorously shipshape; and on the bedside table, a candle, box of matches, snuffer, and a second, spare, candle were laid out in a row, each one an equal distance apart. Pennington, Nathan realized, was destined to grow up into one of those men who lives his life according to timetables, regulations, and petty by-laws; timing by the second, complaining of the insignificant, and correcting other people's grammar and shortcomings to their faces.

Nathan would have dearly loved to turn the room upside down, but what was the use? Pennington would simply order his drudge, Mungbone, to tidy up the mess and make it neat and orderly once more. So instead Nathan contented himself by making a thorough search of Pennington's trunk (which he was surprised to find unlocked) and going through the drawer of his table. Yet in neither place did he come across anything of particular value.

No, Pennington was too shrewd to leave *his* valuables in a spot where they might be easily found. Nathan made a search under his bed where the floor had been recently swept and scrubbed. Again nothing. Nathan didn't suppose there would be, it was far too obvious a place. He thought again and had an idea.

Dropping once more to his knees he searched for a loose floorboard. At last part of one came up in his hands: although he shouldn't have, Nathan felt a glow of satisfied pleasure. He had discovered Pennington's secret hiding-place.

The rest couldn't have been easier. Reaching into the gap between the floor and the ceiling below, Nathan quickly fished out a number of unimportant things: a tin of biscuits, tea, sugar, candied fruits, which Pennington obviously had no intention of sharing. Then he retrieved a little bundle wrapped up in velvet. He carried it to the window and by candle-light unbound it. Inside were six shillings and a pistol with a mother of pearl handle which, as Nathan remembered, Pennington liked to strut around with like some self-important little general.

All these things Nathan stuffed into his pocket. He replaced the food and the loose board and slipped away into his own room. Carefully he hid Pennington's hoard inside his mattress.

'There, Uncle Jago,' he said bitterly, sitting on the edge of his bed. 'I hope you are proud of what I have done for you.'

It was strange, but over the following days Nathan had a strong sense of his uncle's brooding shadow hanging over the school—and nowhere was it more deeply cast than in the woodland. Nathan had no clear idea where Jago was camped out but supposed it was somewhere among the trees, where he'd be skulking like a travelling vagabond. The thought of coming face to face with him was enough to prevent Nathan roaming there at night, and he never felt truly safe unless he was locked away in Mr Gentleman's tower. At the same time, a shocking rumour was going about that there was a thief at Moonville . . .

'Hilliam,' said Mungbone, sidling up in his typically quiet way and speaking softly—in his hand a jug of hot water for Pennington's morning wash. 'There's an odd kind of fellow at the kitchen door asking to see you. Says he used to know your people.'

'*How* odd?' asked Nathan, at once on his guard.

'His hat mainly,' answered Mungbone thoughtfully. 'Can they really be dead mice hanging from it d'you think?'

Nathan didn't reply; he simply turned, bolted upstairs, grabbed the velvet bundle and stuffed it into his shirt. Then he thundered down the stairs—clearing two or three steps at a time—and sped to the kitchen.

Jago was leaning against the doorpost allowing Nip to sniff his fingers and might have been a passing tramp begging for food. Hearing Nathan approach, he looked up and grinned, revealing he was no beggar but the true master of the situation.

'Why, Master *Sam*,' he said. 'I was just on me way by and thought I'd pay me respects to you. Care to take a stroll about the grounds and talk about old times?'

Before he could attract further attention, Nathan hurried him and his dog across the cobbled yard of the stable block, through the overgrown gardens and into the woods.

'Well, what did you get me, boy?' snarled Jago, snatching the bundle from Nathan as soon as he took it out, and spilling its contents on the ground. Nathan saw his eyes narrow as he violently shook the velvet cloth, fully expecting something else to fall down.

'This all?'

Nathan nodded.

Suddenly the back of Jago's hand flew up and Nathan, catching it unprepared, staggered backwards cupping his cheek. Jago glowered down at him, menace brimming over in his voice and his every word tipped with poison.

'Don't you take me for no fool, Nat,' he roared. 'A few coins and a schoolboy's pistol! These are rich men's brats whose fathers pay dear for 'em to learn slothful ways—and don't you tell me 'tis otherwise!'

'I did my best, Uncle.'

'Best! Best!' spat Jago. 'You ain't got no best, Nat, and the sooner I takes you back to your rightful home and beats you into true Blint shape the better.'

His hand sprang up to strike again but remained poised in the air, eventually drifting down to scratch the whiskers along his jaw, his expression softening into thoughtfulness.

Nip whimpered.

'I mean to get me something out of this, Nattie boy, beyond a few trinkets. And I shall. Meet me outside that fine school of yours at three o'clock t'morrow before the sun gets up. I'll expect you there without fail.'

He said no more but reached down and picked up the shillings and Pennington's gun, slipping them inside the torn lining of his coat.

FOURTEEN

Nathan fled to the tower, his face streaked with tears of
rage; and firmly locking the door behind him he threw
himself down and sobbed and sobbed until no more
tears would flow and his eyes were dry and swollen.
Then, overtaken by weariness, he abruptly fell asleep.

He slept and dozed for a long time, feeling feverish
and sweating, while his dreams when they came were
troubled.

He awoke properly at six o'clock and sat up, dry-
washing his face in his hands, his head groggy from too
much sleep. He was not in the least hungry but finding
some dry biscuits and sugar cubes forced himself to
make a meal of them, otherwise it meant he hadn't eaten
all day.

As he chewed the last tasteless biscuit he was startled
to hear someone call out for him.

'Sam! Sam! Where are you?' came the distant voice
from the gardens.

Nathan wriggled uncomfortably. 'Oh please, Richie,
go away and leave me,' he murmured, feeling even more
wretched. 'I'll only drag you down with me.'

Slowly it grew dark, and becoming restless, Nathan
paced between two pale wands of moonlight that angled
down to the floor from the high, narrow windows. Yet
despite his troubles he remembered to attend to Mr
Gentleman's rockets—telling himself sharply he would
keep *that* promise if nothing else.

Midnight . . . one o'clock . . . two o'clock . . . the
hours were slow to chime. Five past . . . quarter past . . .
half past . . . Nathan watched each minute like a miser
who despises his meanness.

Finally at ten minutes to three he set off to meet his uncle, wondering all the time what Jago had planned and feeling sick inside for whatever it was. It was cold now and Nathan shivered, slipping down the side of the darkened school, then being careful to make his way along the grass verge beside the gravel drive so his feet didn't crunch the stones. Creeping through the gate he emerged onto a road magically silver with moonlight.

He heard a low owl call and turned his head. Jago was standing easy against the trunk of a tree, his face pale and his wry smile as uneven as a crack in a dish. Nathan reluctantly crossed to him and Nip growled an unfriendly greeting until Jago seized his muzzle; then Nip knew better than to make a sound, even a whimper of pain.

'Right on time, Nattie,' murmured Jago. 'Though the moonshine goes bad against us.'

Nathan saw that his uncle held an empty sack and from inside his jacket poked a jemmy—a bent iron bar for forcing open windows. Now Nathan had long since known that amongst villains a jemmy was a necessary tool of the trade, yet it was not needed to enter the school for its doors were never locked (which naturally didn't prevent boys from climbing up the ivy to the dormitories for the sheer fun of it)—so why would a jemmy be required tonight?

'Them's a rum pair,' said Jago as if reading his thoughts. 'Him as poor as a mouse that has to pawn its own tail, and her with the air of a snooty duchess.'

Nathan realized he was speaking of the Bentbeefs.

'Lot of nice things hoarded in that house, mind. Worth a man's trouble to take a closer look—*a man or boy*.'

Nathan stared at him. 'Is that it?' he said furiously. 'I have to be a burglar for you now. And worse—a burglar who robs someone he knows. I won't do it, y'hear—'

'You do as you's told, Nattie, or so help me I'll declare who you really are in front of the whole damn school.' And seizing Nathan's collar Jago roughly frog-marched him down the moonlit lane.

Beside him trotted Nip, wagging his stubby tail and finding much malicious pleasure in the misery of his old enemy.

Mr Bentbeef's house, like the school, stood all in darkness at that hour, and before it lay Mrs Bentbeef's well-tended garden, with tall spikes of flowers supported by sticks and the dead-headed roses thrusting up new buds.

Although the flowers appeared in shades of grey they richly coloured the air with scent; and to Nathan's immense irritation, he saw Jago pause to pick himself a carnation for his buttonhole.

Moments later they arrived at the side of the house where the windows were tall and the sills stuck out level with Nathan's head. Jago thrust the empty sack at him and worked the jemmy under the sash of the first window to make a lever. Then he pulled. He pulled until his hat tilted and the hung mice rested on his shoulders as if the little creatures were asleep. He pulled until his hands were slipping, greasy with sweat. Then the frame gave a creak and there was a rumble of movement and the sash rose. The newly made gap was just wide enough for Nathan to squeeze through.

'I'll hoik you aboard,' said Jago, making a stirrup of his hands. Nathan put his foot into it and gripped the sill with one hand and steadied himself on Jago's shoulder with the other, his free foot scraping against the wall. He felt Jago lift him higher, then, almost casually, toss him through the opening. With more sound than was wise, Nathan slithered across the highly polished wooden floor, coming to rest at the foot of Mrs Bentbeef's dining-table.

As he lay there, still and panting for breath, he heard Jago hiss, 'Silver is best, Nat—china'll only break. Fine clocks fetch an 'andsome price if you can find their key. Use your eye, boy, use your eye: pretty things please over all.'

Nathan got to his feet clutching the empty sack. The only light in the room entered through the same window as he had done, for he had clumsily pushed aside the heavy curtains with his fall. His presence stirred the air so that Mrs Bentbeef's gleaming white tags slowly twirled; and Nathan had the unpleasant sensation that they were warning him in the same way they warned her wretched, penniless husband.

'Fill the sack, Nat, fill the sack,' urged Jago watching him.

Nathan edged across to a mahogany show-case made in the form of a Chinese temple. Inside was a collection of stuffed animals, from little birds to a fully grown vixen and her four cubs, all close together as if they lived that crowded way in the wild. Nathan studied them and found his eyes strongly drawn to a polecat raised up on its back legs in a kind of frozen victory dance. Then, shuddering with horror, he noticed the tiny vole clamped between the creature's pitiless jaws.

'Poor little thing,' he said in a sad, solemn voice. 'That's how it is when there's no one to protect you.'

'Eh, Nattie—what's that?' whispered Jago harshly.

As if waking from a dream too soon, Nathan's head began to spin faster and faster. The stuffed animals now reminded him of the seaside waxworks, the glassy-eyed freaks and villains . . .

' . . . and this un 'ad 'er 'ead chopped oft, as did that un . . . ' At the same time a numbing panic rose from his legs and burned hot across his brow. *What on earth was he doing here?* . . . He felt the darkness rub against him like the puma prowling its cage at Colonel Crombie's circus.

No longer acting with any reason, Nathan leapt back from the imagined creature and struck the table. He struck it hard, knocking over a solid silver fruit dish. It landed on its side and began its long roll across the table top. It rolled so slowly that it was almost too painful to watch its progress. Then, at the table's edge, it tottered a moment and fell to the floor. Nathan winced at the harsh noise it made upon the bare wood, ringing up clearly through the house and going on and on as it bounced, like an alarm bell, until Nathan could stand it no longer and covered his ears with his hands.

'You fool, Nat!' he heard Jago rage. 'You fool! Grab what you can and we'll be gone.'

But Nathan never moved. He stared in stupid disbelief at the dish now gleaming and still upon the dark polished floor.

'Be quick, boy—you hear? You wan' 'em to put you away?'

Around him Nathan felt the air grow tense.

Urgent feet sounded on the stairs; whispers on the landings above. Slowly and with effort Nathan gathered his wits about him and turned to face the door leading off into the hallway. A strengthening light flickered under it and, as if it were something harmful, he backed away towards the window. Jago grabbed him as soon as he was in reach and Nathan was half dragged through the opening when Rose came bursting in, dressed in her nightgown and brandishing a poker high above her head.

'Thieves! Highwaymen! Robbers! *M-urderers!*'

Her piercing scream pursued Nathan as he fled through the back vegetable garden, trampling the neat green rows and smashing aside the sticks tied up like wigwams for the peas and beans. Behind him came Jago and Nip, Jago gulping for breath and cursing Nathan at every step.

Nathan was quickly over the fence and away into the woodland.

'Don't you leave me here to struggle, damn you!' roared Jago.

Nathan didn't stop. He couldn't. The only thought in his head was to be as far away from that place as possible.

FIFTEEN

Nathan awoke with a jolt surprised to find his cheek pressed against the earth and the taste of leaf-mould in his mouth. He lay staring up at the underside of trees in a part of the woods he did not know. The night had passed but not the memory of it; Nathan remembered everything coldly and clearly, even when he tried not to. The only part he was unable to recall was falling asleep, which he supposed he must have done when running grew pointless.

He sat up, the arm on which he had slept numb and stiff. He vigorously rubbed it, all the while aware that something had awoken him. A moment later he realized what. It was the school bell, which usually only tolled on Sundays to warn the boys not to fire their guns because it was the Sabbath, and to remind them to collect their Bibles from the dusty corners where they had lain since the previous Sunday; it kept on ringing while they made their way to the village church. There Mr Bentbeef counted them in and counted them out again after the service, for it was not unknown for boys to escape a weekly dose of religion by climbing out of a window.

By this time Nathan was up on his feet, brushing himself down and spitting out the taste of dirt. The urgent bell rang on, and, suddenly curious, he set off to find out why, soon coming across a path to follow. The morning mist had strayed from the fields, drifting through the trees, and beneath its cover he knew anything might lie in wait for him: yet Nathan no longer feared Jago. Strangely, it was his first sighting of the schoolhouse which brought him an unexpected sense of foreboding—the feeling growing stronger the nearer he got to it.

A boy was in the garden and Nathan recognized him as Mungbone, hurrying in with Pennington's shirt previously put out to air. Nathan called to him.

'What's happening?' he asked.

A moth fluttered out of Mungbone's collar. 'Don't you know?' he said in breathless disbelief. 'There's been a robbery at Beefy's house. The thief was caught practically red-handed—and as it turns out he's a boy from this very school.'

'One of the boys . . . caught?' said Nathan stupidly. 'Are you sure? *Quite* sure? Perhaps there has been a mistake.'

Mungbone shook his head. 'Oh no, it's been proven beyond doubt,' he said softly. 'Apparently the maid glimpsed a boy wearing the Moonville uniform and later his penknife was found at the scene. Now Beefy demands that the whole school goes in to the refectory where the boy is to be publicly disgraced.'

'And . . . and who is the boy?' asked Nathan.

Mungbone shrugged. 'Yet just imagine the shame of it. They say Beefy is refusing to involve the law to avoid a scandal, but the fellow is bound to be expelled and the black mark will hang over him for the rest of his life.'

Just then the summoning bell stopped ringing and was followed by a tense silence.

'I must go,' said Mungbone hurrying away. 'I'll be late and Pennington must be bawling for his shirt by now.'

Nathan stood thinking over Mungbone's words before reluctantly joining the last few stragglers making for the Great Hall, slipping into their places behind the long wooden tables. Nathan was too late to sit in his usual seat and squeezed in elsewhere. He was struck by the silence around him: the rowdiness of a normal gathering

100

of boys often made him feel dizzy, but now there wasn't so much as a scrape, cough, or whisper.

All eyes were directed at the raised platform at the far end where Lavender and the other seniors sat to dine. This morning, however, they stood like guards in a line in front of the platform, with Lavender himself deeply serious in a dark morning coat, his hands clasped firmly behind him. On the platform stood an armchair taken from the Bentbeefs' house (Nathan spotted the tell-tale white tag, so he knew) and Mrs Bentbeef dressed in funeral black was seated in it gazing above the boys' heads, her mouth suitably puckered in disdain. Behind the chair hovered Rose as sour and unsmiling as her mistress and still clutching the poker in her hand!

So thick was the silence in the hall that when a side door on to the platform unexpectedly opened, Nathan jumped. From the passageway beyond it arose a boy's voice.

'But Mr Bentbeef, sir, I tell you it wasn't me. It wasn't . . . '

The boy was unrecognizable from his voice, which was hoarse from endlessly protesting his innocence.

Then at the door appeared Mr Bentbeef in his academic gown, yanking the squirming boy by his ear. At that moment every eye was upon the boy; even Mrs Bentbeef condescended to glower his way and Rose was her equal if fierceness was a thing to be measured.

Throughout the length of the hall only one person turned away and that person was Nathan, sick at the injustice of the scene. The boy who honestly claimed his innocence was his best friend, Richie. And Nathan felt a new wave of sickness sweep over him as he remembered how he had borrowed Richie's distinctive penknife, which must have fallen from his pocket during the break-in.

'Silence, sir!' roared Mr Bentbeef. 'Loathsome creature that y'are. Would you add these wicked falsehoods to your growing list of crimes? Silence, I say, and stand where all may gaze upon your dishonest face and know you for what you are.'

'*Villain*,' spat Mrs Bentbeef through narrowed lips.

'*Scoundrel*,' added Rose.

'Aye, *villainous scoundrel*,' raged Mr Bentbeef. 'To think such a viper nestled in our bosom. A scorpion. An unnatural, unfeeling, devious monster!'

'*Monster*,' agreed Mrs Bentbeef and Rose, shaking their heads vigorously.

Richie wrung his hands, his lip trembled and his eyes were glazed with tears. Nathan felt sure he was looking straight at him, appealing to him for friendship's sake to do something.

'Now, sir, stand before me at me table,' ordered Mr Bentbeef. 'Observe, and tell me what I do.'

Miserably Richie obeyed, a moment later saying, 'Y-you're writing, s-sir.'

'*Writing*, indeed I am, sir,' said Mr Bentbeef, his voice clear and indignant as Richie's was small and trembling. 'What is it I write?'

Richie raised himself slightly. 'My n-name, I b-believe, sir.'

'Now, see—quick,' cried Mr Bentbeef excitedly. 'What is it I do, hey?'

Blinking back his tears, Richie said, 'Sc-scratching out m-my name, sir, with your p-pen.'

'Pre-cisely. You, boy, are a blot on an otherwise clean sheet. The sheet is Moonville and you are the blemish upon her fair face.'

'A stain!' bellowed Mrs Bentbeef, staring ahead.

'Now, boy,' continued her husband, working himself up into a new passion. 'What am I writing underneath, hey—hey?'

Richie didn't answer, not directly, but waited for Mr Bentbeef to finish writing, which he did with a savagely stabbed full-stop. Then, slowly, he read aloud, 'Mr B-Bentbeef's Eleventh Commandment: A th-thief shall have no other n-name but THIEF and all shall t-turn their backs . . . and sp-spurn him.'

'Spurn him!' emphasized Mr Bentbeef. 'Such wickedness as yours should not be lost in mumbles but shouted out to the world!'

Taking his newly written sign, Mr Bentbeef hung it around poor Richie's neck; and while he did this Rose marched forward to ram a pointed dunce's cap on to Richie's head, which instead of having the usual D for Dunce had a red T for Thief.

Still his humiliation did not end there. At Mr Bentbeef's insistence a small table was brought on to the platform and a chair set upon it.

'You, sir, will stand upon this seat,' said Mr Bentbeef, 'and there you shall remain until I give word for you to stand down. Then you will wear this hat and sign at all times, yet live apart from other, *decent* boys in case you pollute the very air that they breathe with your vileness. Meantime and without delay I shall write to your parents instructing them to come and remove you from our presence.'

'The sooner the better,' sniffed Mrs Bentbeef.

'And the further the happier we'll be,' added Rose.

Holding the cumbersome cap in place, Richie wearily pulled himself up on to the unsteady chair; and when he stood again tears rolled down his face and splashed upon the table top. Such a wave of ill-feeling for him ran down the hall that all at once the boys took their stale bread rolls and hurled them at him—some striking Mr Bentbeef and his wife—with the greedy or less morally troubled boys taking a bite from theirs first.

Then everyone turned around and no one stared at

Richie any longer but at Nathan, who had not only leapt up but had leapt up upon his table, where he had given such a bellow that the cat-calling had instantly died to be replaced by a wondering silence.

Certain of the hall's attention, Nathan glared about him, fiercely meeting anyone's eye. 'I won't have you be unkind to Richie a moment longer,' he said in a commanding voice. 'He is completely blameless in this matter. If you want your thief, Mr Bentbeef, look no further than me. It is I who tried to rob your house last night, not Richie.'

'Impudent pup,' huffed the headmaster.

'Why, I bet it was you, Hilliam, who stole my gun and shillings too,' scowled Pennington, suddenly appearing on the table before him.

Nathan had no troubled feelings on Pennington's account, so when Pennington made a move to grab him, Nathan knocked him down with a single punch, leaping over him as he lay winded and doubled up at his feet.

And before anyone else could challenge him, he ran down the hall, leaping from one table to the next, kicking over plates and mugs until, with his final jump, he landed on the platform before Richie, who had taken off the pointed cap and was turning it awkwardly in his hands.

'Please don't hate me too much, Richie,' he pleaded, 'I never meant you to come to any harm. I'm not really so bad, you know . . . One day you may find out the whole true story for yourself.'

Behind him the hall stirred like a nest of angry ants.

'Shame on you, Hilliam!' called someone.

'Let *him* wear the thief's cap instead,' insisted someone else.

Nathan gazed up at Richie, hardly knowing what he should do.

But Richie did. He suddenly crumpled up the humiliating cap and threw it on the floor, leaping down himself the next instant and landing on it with both feet.

'Heavens, Sam, don't just stand there staring at me,' he cried. '*Run* and don't let 'em see our heels for dust.'

Briefly startled by his determination, Nathan sprang forward and chased after him to the door—on the way side-stepping Beefy who held out his arms like a boastful fisherman, only to grab air and tumble back into his wife's lap. Then they were racing down a corridor and bursting out through a back door (making sure it was locked behind them).

Richie was breathless and exhilarated. 'Where to now?' he asked.

'The woods,' said Nathan, saying the first thing that came into his head. But as they sped past the stables someone stepped out of the shadows and grabbed them both, throwing them to the ground.

'Still running away, eh, Nattie?' said a voice. And looking up, Nathan saw it was Jago.

SIXTEEN

'Who is this odd creature?' whispered Richie, a little afraid.

'My uncle—Jago Blint—who forced me into becoming a thief,' answered Nathan; and he glanced up at Jago, bristling with defiance.

'There's nothing you can do to hurt me now, Uncle,' he said, his voice assured. 'I've told them everything at the school, they know the truth. Oh, it looks bad—bad for both of us. You best do what you can to save yourself, Uncle, while you still have the time.'

He watched a befuddled expression cross Jago's face as he collapsed on to the edge of a stone trough; and when Nip whimpered and crawled up to him, resting his muzzle on Jago's knee, Jago absently and clumsily stroked his head. Then he brought out a bottle and took an angry swig from it: by the look of him Nathan guessed he had been drinking hard for most of the morning.

'*Told 'em*,' repeated Jago in stung disbelief. 'Why you go and do that for, Nat? You shouldn't have done that. Ah, but don't you worry none, we'll give 'em a fine run for their money, ha! see if we don't. And if they come too close—' From an inside pocket he took out Pennington's pistol, laying it meaningfully across his lap.

Nathan stared at him, horrified. 'Go with you, Uncle?' he said. 'Don't you understand? I'm never going anywhere with you again. I'd rather be dead than be a vermin catcher's apprentice.'

He knew this was a dangerous thing to say, especially with Jago armed and as full of drink as he was.

Jago scowled. 'Soft, Nat, that's your trouble. Soft.

Softer still since you managed to worm a way into this place. This *school*. But one way or another you're coming with me, Nat. *D'y' 'ear?* You're comin' 'ome.'

He rose unsteadily, waving the pistol before him.

'Oh, is he going to shoot us?' murmured Richie much alarmed.

It did appear that they faced extreme danger of one sort or another, but then a new voice spoke, addressing them all.

'Now here's as unpleasant a scene as I've witnessed during all of my travels,' it said. 'And bless me if it isn't taking place on my very own doorstep.'

A great shudder of relief ran through Nathan's body, seeing that the speaker was Mr Gentleman, newly arrived from the railway station.

'Be careful—he has a gun,' warned Nathan.

'To be sure—to be sure,' continued Mr Gentleman pleasantly. 'But I think the fellow too intelligent to fire it.' He turned to Jago as if pleased to meet him. 'Gentleman's the name,' he said, doffing his hat and nodding his head. 'I would shake your hand but it seems rather full at present.'

'I don't need your name or care anything for you,' growled Jago in return. 'I've come to take the boy away and *you* can go to the devil.'

'In which case,' said Mr Gentleman quietly, 'I shall require flames.'

As he spoke, his hand slipped in and out of his pocket—then he dashed something hard on the cobbles. There was a brilliant white flash followed by much confusion. Nip yelped and Jago roared and Mr Gentleman shouted, 'To the tower!'

Of course the flash had been caused by one of Mr Gentleman's lightning bombs, but it stunned Richie as much as Jago for whom it was intended. Grabbing his friend's arm, Nathan yanked him to his feet. Then all

107

three of them were running—running even faster when a bullet whistled low over their heads.

Nathan, who had the key, let them into the tower and followed them up the stone stairs and through the second door, into the circular library room.

Mr Gentleman immediately threw off his coat and rushed away to fetch brandy. He poured a measure for both boys ('Shock,' he said) and steered them towards a couch.

'Sit here and drink,' he said. 'No—no, sip it,' he added when Richie took a deep gulp and began to cough and his eyes began to stream. Turning then to Nathan, Mr Gentleman regarded him calmly, saying, 'Now suppose you tell me what this business is all about, Sam.'

Nathan looked up and faced him squarely. 'To begin with, Mr Gentleman,' he said, 'my name is not Sam Hilliam. It never has been. The truth of the matter is my name is Nathan Wheatear . . . '

Even Richie stared at him then.

Mr Gentleman listened long and hard to all that Nathan had to say (which really was the story of his life), and as he listened he endlessly paced up and down. He didn't interrupt, not once. Nor did Richie, who wriggled with unanswered questions; but at the moments when his astonishment grew too much to contain he'd murmur 'Heavens'. As for Nathan, now he had begun he found he couldn't stop, his story like a runaway cart which he was determined to ride out to the finish. Speaking so openly and honestly made him feel almost light-headed, never before realizing just how heavily burdened he had been by his deceit.

He ended by giving an account of what had happened that very morning; and when he was done he sat trying to guess how Mr Gentleman and Richie would judge him. They were both very quiet, Richie shooting him little reassuring glances: yet Nathan found Mr Gentleman's continued silence *most* worrying. At last he stopped pacing.

'What you have done is wrong, child—very wrong indeed,' he said, and in such a solemn voice that Nathan's face dropped in dismay. 'Yet,' he continued, 'could I honestly claim that I would have acted any differently in the same situation? And in your defence it must be added that you did not steal your new identity, it was freely given to you by its rightful owner—'

'But I *am* still a thief, Mr Gentleman,' argued Nathan. 'A thief in its worst possible sense.'

'No, not a thief,' said Mr Gentleman, 'but the unwilling servant to a thief—this Jago Blint—undoubtedly the true rogue of this sorry affair. Your honesty in fact does you credit, it saved your friend here from complete disgrace. Anything else may be quickly forgiven or overlooked by all save the smallest minded.'

Richie finished off his brandy. 'I say A-men to that,' he said happily and perhaps a little drunk.

Nathan was less easily convinced. 'If only you were a judge or Mr Bentbeef,' he said.

'Why? You told us yourself, Sa—*Nathan*, I mean.' For the first time Mr Gentleman allowed himself a smile. 'You told us yourself that Mr Bentbeef refuses to involve the law and, if Mr Bentbeef is as you make him out to be, I think he will be quite happy for me to recompense him for any damage or inconvenience.'

'You will do that for me?' said Nathan genuinely astonished.

'Why yes, I can't lose you now, boy, you're quite invaluable to me as my assistant.'

'Assistant?'

'Of course. Haven't you realized? I've been training you for the part for many weeks now. You escaped your uncle to acquire an education; well you have been receiving one, although admittedly not from Mr Bentbeef's establishment where you thought it would come. I would very much like you to stay and work alongside me here at the tower—that is, if you will agree to the arrangement.'

'Me? Living at the tower?' Nathan leapt up. 'Why, yes. Yes. Yes! Of course I agree to it. There is nothing I wish more—' Then slowly he sank back down on to the couch. 'But what about my Uncle Jago?' he asked. 'You'll never buy him off as easily as Mr Bentbeef.'

As if in answer to his name, the door suddenly rattled and a rough voice shouted, 'Nat! Nat! I know you're in there. You come out, boy—you come out and face me; I'm taking you home.'

Richie jumped back in alarm. 'How ever did he manage to get through the outside door?' he wondered.

'Easy,' said Nathan. 'He picked the lock.'

'Well, he won't get into this room,' said Mr Gentleman confidently. 'There is no lock to pick but a metal bolt that is strong enough to keep out an army.'

He made to cross to the door but Nathan grabbed his jacket tail. 'Don't let him in, Mr Gentleman,' he pleaded. 'He's been drinking and you cannot be sure of what he'll do.'

'Still, I must speak to the fellow,' replied Mr Gentleman, and he went over to the door.

'You—Jago Blint,' he called. 'There is nothing here for you, you scoundrel. Quickly be on your way.'

Jago struck the door with his fist. 'And who might you be to tell *me* to be on me way? Oh, I knows your name right enough—but *who* are you?'

'Never you mind, Blint. It's enough to know that I am a friend of your nephew and no friend of yours. Go away before I inform the authorities of your whereabouts and crimes.'

'I'll go soon as I has what is rightfully mine and belongs elsewhere, not here to no stranger. Hand me the boy, I say!'

'Nathan stays here with me. I undertake to bring him up as you can not. That is also his free choice in the matter.'

'*Free choice*,' sneered Jago. From the far side of the door arose the sound of rummaging, then something came sliding beneath it. A scrap of old parchment. Nathan stared at it, recognizing at once the royal licence granted to the Blint family centuries before.

'You sound an educated man. You read this. Nat's a Blint. He follows in a line. Nobody can have him except me. Me! Jago Blint.'

'Go away, man. Can't you see you're only making more—'

Suddenly Mr Gentleman leapt back—the dark wood of the door had split open, revealing pale splinters where a bullet now lodged.

Unable to reason against a weapon, Mr Gentleman hurried back to safety and looked so shaken that Nathan poured him another brandy.

'I warned you,' he whispered, as if Jago might overhear. 'He'll never give me up. *Never*. I best go with him quietly. At least that way you and Richie won't get hurt.'

'The scoundrel.' Ignoring his own advice, Mr Gentleman downed the brandy in one and said, 'Rest assured, Nathan, you're going nowhere with a monster like that.'

'So what do we do?' demanded Richie. He frowned thoughtfully. 'I suppose we might try raising help from the boys.'

'If they would want to come to our help,' said Nathan gloomily. 'In any case I expect most of them have galloped off to the woods to hunt us down.'

111

'But there must be another way of getting out of here,' said Richie gazing around at the bookshelves.

Mr Gentleman shook his head. 'I'm afraid not. The only other way has been firmly blocked off. All I can suggest is that we sit tight and let the fellow rant and rave as much as he likes in the hope that drink finally overtakes him and he falls asleep.'

Nathan was not convinced it was going to be as simple as that where Jago was concerned. Still, along with the others he tried to behave as if nothing was wrong, despite Jago cursing and battering at the door—and sometimes firing off his gun in pure frustration. Then it grew silent—worryingly so in Nathan's view.

'Perhaps the villain is asleep now,' said Mr Gentleman listening.

'I doubt it,' said Nathan. 'He'll be far too angry for that.'

Suddenly Richie said, 'I can smell smoke. Yes look! It's coming in from under the door.'

Mr Gentleman raced across to it. 'What on earth are you doing, man?' he called.

And Jago answered coolly, 'Ain't I just smoking out vermin, sir . . . Ain't I just doing me job.'

Nathan saw Mr Gentleman shake his head and understood why. The fire was burning dangerously close to the little room where the gunpowder and firewood was stored.

Mr Gentleman said grimly, 'If the flames take a hold the whole tower will go off like a primed bomb—with us in it.'

'Lor', must we surrender to him then?' asked Richie, and he was startled by Nathan's unexpected shout.

'What an idiot I am,' he laughed. 'I know how we can get away and Jago can do nothing about it. Come on, follow me!'

SEVENTEEN

Poor old Mr Gentleman and Richie hardly had time to exchange puzzled glances before they decided it was best not to be left behind.

Up and up, through the shelves of books they raced, Nathan already several levels higher; and as he led the way he felt secretly pleased with himself for only he knew where to go and why. There wasn't a moment to waste on explanations (not yet anyway): thickening orange smoke was rising faster than they could run, and was fouling the air; besides, Mr Gentleman was wheezing too much to manage a single questioning word.

Finally, reaching the top of the tower, Nathan stood waiting impatiently for them by the disguised door—which he had opened in readiness.

'That is just an old cupboard,' protested Mr Gentleman, arriving last and breathless on the scene.

'No cupboard can do what this can,' replied Nathan, still holding the secret tantalizingly before them. 'Now inside and be careful, it's going to be very crowded.' And a moment later, when they had crushed themselves inside, he shouted, 'Here, Richie—help me work this lever, will you. Not yet! Mr Gentleman, kindly close the door behind you. *Now*, Richie; and watch what happens.'

Just as before when the lever was moved to and fro, the floor began to rise and the ceiling open but, unlike before, when there was just Nathan to marvel at this mechanical wonder, this time there was Richie and Mr Gentleman too.

At last the ceiling was fully opened out and the floor had reached roof level.

'Can't you guess what it is yet?' asked Nathan teasingly. And when he received only blank looks in return, he said, 'This is where Sir Humphrey launched his balloon—and all his equipment is still here for us to use.'

'Balloon?' repeated Richie looking no less blank. But Mr Gentleman understood at once.

'I thought all that had been destroyed years ago,' he said.

'Not destroyed—lost,' said Nathan. 'But before we can do anything with it we must first be rid of the clutter that stands in our way. Quickly, over the side with it!'

A few minutes of frantic activity followed—with crate after crate going over the side and crashing to earth below; and from the smashed-up pieces there flew a confusing blizzard of papers, blowing in every direction.

Suddenly Nathan gave a shout: 'No, Richie, not those!' Just in time he had caught his friend, who had gathered up a pair of canvas pipes and was about to throw them away. 'We shall need those to carry the balloon gas from the tanks,' explained Nathan. 'And see that wicker basket over there? That has to be turned upside down and emptied to make room for us to ride in. Oh do hurry—the smoke is getting thicker by the minute.'

This was true. Dense, bitter-tasting smoke was leaking out of every tiny gap in the top of the tower. Hurriedly they laid out the skin of the balloon and joined it, as they thought it was meant to go, to the wicker basket. Then Nathan connected the canvas pipes to the tanks of balloon gas. It required all his effort to move both valves and then a loud hissing arose. At the same time the balloon skin started to billow and wriggle like a sack of bad-tempered foxes.

Down on the ground, meanwhile, Jago was taking

114

particular malicious pleasure from his wickedness. The smoke and heat had driven him back bit by bit, until at last he stood a distance away from the tower, half concealed by bushes.

'There, Nattie,' he whispered to himself. 'Let your fine words get you out of this. Believe me, you ain't going to blab your tale to no one, save Saint Peter and his angels.' Then Nip gave a small, uneasy growl. A large mysterious ball was taking shape amidst the smoke and rising up from the tower's roof. Jago saw it too and watched with intense suspicion. Was it possible he was about to be cheated?

His howl of rage sent the rooks cawing from their nests.

The fire was taking hold at an extraordinary rate. On the roof top—as busy as they all were—Nathan and the others could not block out the distant sound of angry crackling. And for a brief moment the image of flames dancing along shelves of priceless books flickered before Nathan's eyes, filling him with a sense of hopelessness.

But this was not the time to dwell on such matters. The hiss of balloon gas had almost died away: the tanks were fast emptying and the balloon swelled out impressively above their heads, revealing for the first time in many years its design of clouds and blue sky on one side, darkening to night with stars and a great crescent moon on the other.

'Make haste and climb aboard, boys,' shouted Mr Gentleman. 'I doubt there can be many minutes left us.'

'You can't possibly mean into that blessed small thing?' wailed Richie. 'It's hardly bigger than a picnic hamper!'

Nathan grabbed his arm and together they flung themselves into the wicker basket; Mr Gentleman was right behind once he had shut off the two gas valves.

Now came a tricky part. The balloon was moored by a rope, and the rope was attached to a winch which was firmly bolted to the tower. Briefly Mr Gentleman explained that in Sir Humphrey's day two strong men were employed to wind out the rope and wind it back again after Sir Humphrey had finished his sky-watching. A metal peg through the cogs of the winch acted as a brake.

'Pull that out,' said Mr Gentleman, 'and I dare say the balloon will rise like a cork in water.'

Nathan saw it fell to him to remove it: he was taller than Richie, while it was out of the question even to consider Mr Gentleman. So with Richie and Mr Gentleman hanging on to his legs he leaned further and further out of the basket towards the peg.

'I've got it,' he finally gasped.

'Then give it a good tug, Nat,' said Richie.

Nathan did. It came out surprisingly easily, and with a stomach-churning jolt the balloon bobbed up, carrying its three passengers skywards.

Nathan found himself hastily clawed back on board to safety.

Seconds later a rougher jolt indicated they had reached the rope's limit and now, free of the smoke cloud, the school with its dramatically burning tower became part of a greater view, along with the woodlands and the surrounding Downs.

Observing themselves so high above the fire, Nathan and Richie cheerfully thought the worst part behind them. Only Nathan caught the decidedly worried frown on Mr Gentleman's face.

'What is it?' he asked.

Mr Gentleman wrung his hands. 'It suddenly occurs to me that we have nothing with which to cut the rope and set ourselves free,' he said.

'Do we need to?' asked Richie. 'Surely we are far enough away from the tower now.'

'Not when it blows up and becomes ten thousand flying splinters of stone and wood.'

This, pointed out to them, made their mood once more grim.

'If only I had my penknife here,' Richie couldn't help muttering to himself and Nathan, overhearing, looked away guiltily.

He saw that Mr Gentleman was urgently gathering up the loose strands of rope that hung down from the balloon. 'With a bit of luck, boys, we may be able to ride out the blast,' he said. He shared the rope between them. 'Do the same as me. Wind the rope around yourselves and thread it through the wickerwork. The corners are stronger than the sides. Quickly, quickly now. Make sure you're securely tied in.'

Nathan and Richie did as they were urged, and had just finished when a small muffled explosion was heard way down on the ground.

'Here it comes!' shouted Mr Gentleman.

The next moment the sky was torn apart by a second, stupendous explosion and a flash of searing white light . . . after which Nathan remembered nothing.

It might have been seconds later, or minutes, or even hours. Nathan opened his eyes to see an upside-down world so far above his head that at first he was sluggishly curious. He wondered too why his arms hung loose about him and his legs danced aimlessly in the air—waving like the limbs of a rag-doll.

A distant voice urgently spoke his name. 'Nathan! Nathan!' But it was far too much trouble for him to answer.

'Nathan!' yelled Mr Gentleman again. 'Richie, help me haul him back on board.'

Only then did Nathan realize, to his great shock, that the force of the explosion had thrown him backwards out of the balloon's now rather battered basket and he was hanging upside-down outside it—the rope which had saved his life, cutting into his stomach.

Between them, Richie and Mr Gentleman managed to pull him to safety, afterwards loosening his rope.

'I'm all right,' smiled Nathan, pale and a little unsteady, his ears still ringing from the blast. 'I expect I shall feel less dizzy once I am back on firm ground.'

'I'm afraid you must be patient,' said Mr Gentleman. 'The explosion not only severed the mooring rope, but has sent us soaring. It will take some time before we drift back down.'

'And the balloon, has it been damaged at all?' enquired Nathan, anxiously peering up at the swollen shape.

'Not the skin, thankfully,' replied Mr Gentleman. 'But I cannot work the flap to release the gas; and, of course, we have no means of steering ourselves which leaves us completely at the mercy of the wind.'

Richie obligingly licked his finger and held it up. 'A steady south-westerly,' he announced.

Mr Gentleman shrugged his indifference. 'But how long and how far it will carry us is any man's guess.'

The balloon together with its three reluctant passengers sailed on, and Nathan was indeed surprised to see their distance above the world when he made his first proper survey. Below him everything appeared so tiny—as the balloon itself must have done in the eyes of those who stood watching it from the ground. Searching for the tower he could find no trace of it, but thought perhaps a spindly column of smoke in the distance might mark its remains; and he wondered about Jago and Nip.

Then Richie, standing at his elbow, nudged him and exclaimed, 'Look, Nat!' and pointed at a stately line of geese flying by within feet of them, at exactly the same level as their eyes. He laughed heartily. 'A Moonville boy wouldn't need a gun up here,' he said. 'He could just reach out and grab his dinner. Why, I shouldn't mind a balloon of my own one day.'

However, after an hour confined in that cramped and creaky and alarmingly fragile basket which swung like a giddy fairground ride, Richie's passion for balloon-riding had reached an end. He crouched in a corner complaining of feeling sick and shivering violently whenever the balloon passed through a cloud, each being as damp, cold, and dispiriting as November fog; and his teeth chattered, despite the sun's fierce heat just a few feet away.

Mr Gentleman spoke very little. He had his pocket spy-glass trained on the Downs as the balloon began its long slow descent. Nathan glanced up as suddenly he looked through the spy-glass, lowered it, then raised it to his eye once more. He did it in such a particular way that Nathan asked, 'What do you see?'

'The English Channel,' came the reply. 'Here, take a look for yourself.'

Mr Gentleman handed Nathan his spy-glass and Nathan peered through it, crying out at once, 'I can see a ship! A three-master. And sailors running up its rigging.'

'I sincerely hope none of 'em feel as seasick as me,' groaned Richie, clutching his stomach.

'It's as I feared,' said Mr Gentleman. 'If we continue much further on our present course we shall be blown out to sea. The wind is freshening and we are picking up speed.'

Nathan stared at him blankly. It didn't seem fair to escape the flames only to go down beneath the waves instead.

'At least the main mooring rope is still attached to us,' he said, trying to sound hopeful. 'Perhaps it will catch somewhere.'

119

It was a remote chance. Mr Gentleman took back his spy-glass and scanned below. 'Now,' he said, 'what do you think that can be, there on the road?'

But Nathan leaning out over the basket already had the answer.

'It's a travelling circus!' he cried.

And he knew it was not any old circus either.

EIGHTEEN

'There, that's Colonel Crombie now, riding out in front,' said Nathan, pointing to a figure in a fringed jacket; although his matchless white horse with its proud, high-stepping gait was no less distinctive.

'Are you sure?' asked Mr Gentleman.

'It's Crombie's circus all right,' said Nathan. 'You can't mistake its ringmaster for any other.'

Behind Colonel Crombie rumbled the heavy show-wagons—like great awkward galleons from another age—gleaming and polished and throwing up dust from the dry, chalk road; then came the wheeled cages and then the homely caravans, with various animals, outriders, and strollers scattered down the column's length. The brass band played a military march, seated on tiered seats on top of the leading vehicle, and their instruments and the gold ornament upon their uniforms dazzled the eyes.

'The circus must be travelling to a new pitch,' observed Nathan.

'Can you see Sam Hilliam—the *real* Sam Hilliam?' asked Richie keenly, for he already felt he knew him well despite having never actually met him.

Nathan searched the travelling show again. Then he laughed and pointed. 'There he is!' And Richie and Mr Gentleman saw a small figure riding an elephant, sitting close behind the creature's large, flapping ears, which must have made wonderful fans on such a hot day as this. His fellow rider was a huge strongman outrageously dressed in a tiger skin. The elephant pulled a caravan whose weight meant as little to it as the flies buzzing around its tiny eyes; and the elephant was brightly clad in crimson, complete with a golden tasselled cap.

When the balloon glided into view the band broke off in discord and the circus folk stared up in wonder at the uncommon sight in the sky.

'Ahoy there!' shouted Nathan (which is how they hail each other out at sea and, when all is said and done, what is a balloon but a ship of the air?) 'Can you hear me down below?'

'We can hear you perfectly, friend,' returned Colonel Crombie in his easy drawl, and he doffed his hat uncovering his long corn-gold hair.

'And what of Sam Hilliam? Can he hear me too?'

Nathan saw Sam nearly fall from the elephant in surprise. 'Y-yes, I can hear you, who is it that asks?'

Nathan grinned. 'It's Nathan Wheatear, the boy who went to Moonville in your place.'

'*Nathan Wheatear* . . . impossible,' wailed Sam. 'You were going to be a scholar. *I* was supposed to have all the adventures!'

It pleased Nathan no end to hear the note of envy in his voice.

At this point Mr Gentleman took over because the balloon was drifting out of hailing distance.

'We desperately need your help, Colonel,' he called through cupped hands. 'We're cut loose and in peril of drifting out to sea.'

'How can we be of service?' asked Colonel Crombie.

'If you can catch the main rope and secure it we will be much obliged.'

As he spoke his words grew faint and distant.

Immediately Sam saw a way of joining in Nathan's adventure, and tapping the elephant (whose name was Cassia) on the head, gave her the sign to kneel. As soon as she was down he slipped off her back, unhitched the caravan and raced back to his place beside the strongman.

'Vhat you do?' asked Caspar looking perplexed.

'We're going to rescue Nathan,' answered Sam. 'And we shall probably need all the brute strength we can muster.'

Caspar beamed. Brute strength was what he was best at.

From the air none of this was clear. The picture was more confused. At first Colonel Crombie led the balloon chase across the fields, with a host of circus folk streaming after him on foot or on horseback, but coming to a high flint wall they were forced to change direction in order to find a gate, losing much precious time in the process.

For Cassia, however, arriving upon the scene a moment later, the wall presented no problem at all. She hardly lost a single stride. She simply lowered her head and knocked a hole through it, and stepping free of the dust cloud went romping across the next field, demolishing whatever else stood in her path.

'Sit tight,' called Sam in his old confident way, once Cassia had caught up with the balloon. 'We'll have you down before you know it.'

'Try to catch the rope,' shouted Mr Gentleman.

The old mooring rope trailed the ground. Cassia stalked it in a similar way a kitten stalks a line of wool, or so it appeared to Nathan, and had the circumstances been different he might have laughed aloud with Richie at the novelty of it. As it was, the breeze played the balloon just as the rope seemed to play the elephant, always slipping just out of reach, and if the breeze was not blowing the balloon further away it was lifting it higher, so that Sam and Caspar were forced to make ever more desperate grabs at the frayed rope end.

To the south the sea reappeared, this time not as a glimpsed thing, distant and between hills, but as a broad expanse, gleaming and silver-green—and much closer than ever before. The balloon had reached a high point on the Downs, after which the land sloped gently away, ending abruptly in grey chalk cliffs. Beyond these lay nothing but sea and sky and the wheeling birds that patrolled them.

Suddenly Richie let out a shout. 'They've done it! They've caught the rope.'

Sure enough, Sam had just made a lunge for the rope and now it was tightly gripped in his hands. To his amazement it instantly lifted him off Cassia's shoulders and Caspar, catching the boy by his knees, yanked him back into place. He still held on to the rope, and between them they managed to pull down a sufficient length for Cassia to grasp in her mouth, curling her trunk around it like the tendril of a plant. Afterwards she gave a triumphant if somewhat muffled trumpet.

'Well done, girl,' said Sam, slapping her flank.

Yet the balloon had lost none of its strength, and much to the creature's indignation she found herself now dragged along the ground in an ungainly fashion, forcing up the turf before her into a wrinkled pile like a green rug on a polished floor.

Caspar helped, pulling the rope till not only his muscles stood out but the veins in his neck and arms too. But not even their combined efforts were enough to bring the balloon to a halt.

'The tree! The tree!' shouted Mr Gentleman. 'Tie the rope around its trunk.'

Nathan saw the tree of which he spoke was a dead, wind-stunted poplar standing alone in the middle of a pasture. It was possibly the last tree before France. As Cassia was dragged through a clump of gorse bushes towards it, a group of sheep bolted from its shade and fled in all directions.

Working together as a team and using every last bit of their strength, Cassia and Caspar hauled the balloon low. It dropped only by a few feet, and the effort came close to exhausting them, but won enough free rope for Sam to slip off Cassia's back, wind the rope around the tree trunk and secure it with a knot (the only one he ever mastered when he was determined to run away to sea).

Still this did not amount to a rescue, and the balloon tugged and rocked so much that Nathan, Richie, and Mr Gentleman were thrown together and against the sides like sailors in a storm. As for the old tree, it groaned and creaked and its roots began to rip up from the soil with the same whiplash force as the ropes holding up the Big Top during a hurricane.

'Vhat muss ve do now?' called Caspar, pausing only to brush the sweat from his eyes.

'We need weight to counter the buoyancy. It is the only hope of bringing us back to earth,' answered Mr Gentleman.

'And look,' called Nathan. 'Help's at hand!' For just then Colonel Crombie appeared over the brow of the hill with a posse of clowns, bandsmen, and sparkly entertainers, all running flat out.

Quickly Sam explained to them the problem, which was when Caspar's wife, Sophia, saw how she might play a part. She was a celebrated high-wire walker, and borrowing the saddle-bags from Colonel Crombie's horse, she swiftly filled them with lumps of rock freshly thrown up by the half uprooted tree.

When next Nathan saw her she was steadily climbing the rope towards him with the saddle-bags thrown over her shoulder. He helped Mr Gentleman pull her aboard and she turned to the applauding circus crowd, her arm raised in acknowledgement. Mr Gentleman warmly shook her hand, and she kissed Nathan's cheek and then she kissed Richie.

'Lor',' he said, colouring up.

'There is more to do,' said Sophia, promptly emptying the bags of rubble on to the floor of the basket; and as she disappeared over the side she added, 'Cheerio, dears, I shall be as quick as I can.'

And she was true to her word. While Sam and the rest of the circus company dashed around the field, digging out stone with their bare hands and piling it high in a heap, Sophia carried the stone up the rope two saddle-bag loads at a time and tipped it about the feet of Nathan and his companions.

Soon they stood ankle deep in chalk and flint and the basket's wicker bottom bowed dangerously. Slowly, with each deposit, the balloon sank by a few more inches. But time was running short: the wind was getting up and the old poplar groaned and creaked as never before, fresh roots bursting out of the ground with a violent scattering of soil.

To add to their troubles, Mr Gentleman foresaw a new problem.

'If one of us suddenly leaves the basket,' he said, 'the loss of weight will cause the balloon to rise sharply, and that may be enough to tug the tree's remaining roots from the ground.'

'In that case,' said Nathan, 'we must all three of us leave together.' And he called for Sam to bring up Cassia. 'We need her strong, broad back,' he explained.

When the elephant was manoeuvred into position beneath the balloon, Nathan and his two friends swung their legs over the side of the basket.

'I'll count to three and then we must jump,' said Nathan. 'One . . . Two . . . '

The tree gave a sickening crack and lurch—

' . . . Three!'

Whereupon they dropped from the balloon and fell through the air. It was much higher than Nathan previously imagined. The tree flashed past his eyes, showering dirt on to him; the next instant he landed on

Cassia's back with Mr Gentleman and Richie sprawled beside him, safe and unhurt.

Glancing up, they were just in time to witness the balloon float rapidly away trailing the dead tree as if no more than one of its twigs.

NINETEEN

Long after that eventful day of balloon escapes and rescue by elephant, a letter finally came into Nathan's hands. It was written in furious haste, the handwriting as spiky as the raised hair on an angry dog.

Sir:

If I should address you in such a civil way, which I am led to believe I should not, since you come off the streets like a stray carrying the title 'gentleman' like a bone in your mouth. I wish it known that I consider you the lowest, vilest scoundrel imaginable. To deceive a person of my good standing into the not inconsiderable expense of your unlikely education is beyond the comprehension of all but the blackest of minds. And, let it be further understood, had not my ward, Samuel Hilliam, been part of this wholly incredible scheme, I would have taken steps to notify the constabulary. As it is, the whereabouts of said ward are still not precisely known, but be assured by me he too shall be severely reprimanded for his part in this deceit.

I close this letter not expecting to hear from you or of you again. Do not by any means try to make further claims on my generosity. For my part, I do not ask after your health, wealth, or happiness. I wish you well in no way at all!

Yours,
R. J. Smeasle

Nathan showed his letter to Richie and Sam, who read it by the light of their lanterns.

'Heavens!' exclaimed Richie, handing it back. 'This Mr Smeasle can certainly breathe fire.'

Sam laughed. '*Pah*. This is mild fire to the flames I usually draw out of him,' he said. 'It hardly scorches your finger tips at all.'

'Will you tell him where you are?' asked Nathan.

Sam shrugged. 'Not yet. I'm quite taken with the circus life at present—although I might just drop him a line from time to time to stoke up his coals.'

'Watch your spelling if you do,' said Nathan, which made them laugh all over again.

He had met Richie and Sam by arrangement in the road before Moonville, and now the three of them walked past the broken stump of Mr Gentleman's tower, the scaffolding around it masking the re-building work. Adjoining it, the main block (the school in other words) had escaped the calamity remarkably undamaged. True, tiles had been loosened and many windows shattered, but nothing worse; and better still, no boy or anyone else from the school had been harmed in any way, not even by the slightest scratch.

Five months had now passed since the day of that dreadful explosion. During that time much had happened.

Jago had been caught trying to make his way back to the city and put in prison, and was due to stand trial any day now. (The trial, when it *did* take place, ran for many weeks: Jago had been made totally deaf by the blast he caused and was in need of everything written down. When on the opening day the judge held up a placard with the words 'Does the defendant plead guilty or not guilty?' printed upon it, Jago ripped it to shreds, biting the pieces in his great rage; and Nip ran through the court sinking his teeth into the trouser seats of several barristers and policemen. A very long sentence resulted, the judge so furious with Jago that his wig was askew.)

Despite losing everything, Mr Gentleman with Nathan's assistance insisted on continuing his work, their home and laboratory now a caravan lent by Colonel Crombie until the tower was complete. Mr Gentleman had learned a valuable lesson and this time round he was going to store all his explosives in a different place and an underground chamber was being dug for that purpose. Moreover, he had so deeply impressed Colonel Crombie, who was constantly on the look-out for novelty acts for his circus, that he wasted no time in commissioning Mr Gentleman to build him a replica of Sir Humphrey's balloon, and also rockets to fire off from one of the show-wagons before each performance began. The balloon was used nightly in a gigantic tug-of-war contest, with Caspar and a team of elephants pulling against it—the elephants led by Cassia, dressed in scarlet fringed with gold.

Of course Nathan had been expelled from Moonville, Mr Bentbeef demanding that much. However, when Mr Gentleman agreed to compensate him for the burglary and damage from the explosion, he made one thing clear: Mr Bentbeef would not receive a single penny unless Nathan was allowed to tell the school the entire story of how he came to be there and why he had so nearly robbed its headmaster. Mr Bentbeef huffed and puffed a great deal before grudgingly giving his consent.

Nathan felt nervous standing alone on the platform with so many faces watching him. He eyed the stale bread rolls on the tables and knew the boys would use them as missiles if they still thought badly of him afterwards (Mr Gentleman couldn't protect him from that). He told his tale as well and truthfully as he was able; and then, when it was done, he was dismayed to see the boys dive as one for the bread and throw it as hard as they could. Yet not a single crust or crumb ever touched Nathan. Instead the stone-hard rolls rained down on Mr Bentbeef, accompanied by many jeers, until the little black-clad figure who had stood scowling at the side of the platform was forced to flee, shrieking with terror. And one bread roll—suspiciously from Mungbone's direction—hit hard on the back of Pennington's head nearly knocking him off his bench.

Then Nathan stepped forward and amidst riotous cheers and the hammering of fists and mugs on the boards was carried shoulder-high around the school.

Leaving the school behind, Nathan and his friends walked on through the woods, laughing and talking as they went, until they saw the Downs rolling away below them, the hills and valleys all comfortably rounded and grey in the starlight. The moon in the centre of the sky was only a slither, but the stars appeared more numerous, drifting overhead in wide milky swathes. Ahead, the boys heard voices muttering in low conversation, for many other people had gathered there at the edge of the woods, stamping their cold feet on the hard frosty ground, and all wondering excitedly what was to come. They were a mixture of boys from Moonville and circus folk who camped nearby, plus one or two curious villagers. Everyone was muffled in coats and scarves, and here and there lanterns glowed although out in the open their light was unnecessary; Richie and Sam blew out their own candles so as not to waste them.

The crowd formed an orderly ring around Mr Gentleman, busily adjusting his latest rocket—and what a rocket it was. It stood as high as two tall men, with a body as thick as a young tree; its pointed cap, like the roof of a turret, was directed straight at the stars; and so heavy was the rocket that it required a wooden scaffold simply to hold it upright. Painted down its side was its name. *Sky Piercer*.

After meeting so many fellow planetarians during his visit north, Mr Gentleman had returned to Moonville convinced that if he wanted to talk to the stars he had to 'speak a little louder', and nothing less than a monster rocket would do the trick. Now, after many false starts and experiments, Sky Piercer was ready to launch.

Noticing Nathan's arrival, Mr Gentleman quickly completed his final preparations. 'Stand well clear,' he called. 'And be prepared to shield your eyes.'

The murmuring crowd shuffled back.

Mr Gentleman searched in his pockets and found a box of matches and then began to search again. Nathan knew he needed a taper because a match flame burned too briefly for his purpose, so he helpfully ran forward with Mr Smeasle's letter twisted into a paper wand. Mr Gentleman took it, lit it and held it to the fuse. When certain it was alight he retired to the safety of the crowd.

A white fizzing fire crept along the lengthy fuse, nearer and nearer to the body of the rocket. The crowd followed its every spark, hushed with expectation, their faces lit by the jumping light.

Steadily the spitting fire gobbled up the fuse until it reached the base of the rocket. *Then*—it went dark.

'It's gone out!' wailed Richie. The crowd breathed, in disappointment.

But no. White sparks now appeared, a few insignificant ones at first like the early flakes of a snowstorm, a moment later becoming a showering blizzard of furnace red. Volcano tongues of fire followed, shooting out with such force that they bounced up from the ground, roaring like a dragon. People covered their ears in fright. Others winced and closed their eyes or fled to a safer distance. And in the space of those few busy seconds the rocket whip-lashed into the sky, its trail a straight white line. Behind it a cloud of reeking smoke from the scorched earth rapidly drifted away.

Up and up the rocket went, its trail as straight as ever. Nathan watched, tilting back his head until his nose was higher than his ears. He knew the rocket was climbing to incredible heights, and still it went blazing on through the darkness as if it meant to take itself to the moon—or beyond.

Then, unexpectedly, the climbing stopped and the high breeze-blown trail began fading to ghostly silver. The crowd with no reason to believe otherwise thought this an end, some applauding politely. Nathan knew better. He waited for the final explosion and a moment or two later it came. First a sheet of blinding white light filled half the sky—and from its centre shot some dozen red and green beams whose tips sprouted long blue spines. Then, as these died, there appeared a twinkling of soft pink stars falling through veils of golden dust that slowly dimmed . . . and were gone.

Like an avalanche in a remote valley the boom of the explosion reached them last of all.

Nathan raced forward wanting to be the first to congratulate Mr Gentleman, who calmly checked his chronometer.

'Thirty-two point three-seven seconds,' he announced, quietly triumphant. Then he winked. 'And the next one shall be even better, Nat,' he whispered. 'Between us, boy, we will build a rocket that will scorch its way out of the Earth's atmosphere. Think of it—the very first voyage into Outer Space!'

Instead of shaking his hand, Nathan danced him round and round, only slowly growing aware that no one else had rushed up with him. Sam and Richie along with the rest of the crowd were too busy staring up in wonder at the sky.

Nathan looked up with them.

Four dots of red light had appeared from different points of the compass and were rushing to meet each other at unthinkable speed across the shining galaxy. And, just when it seemed to Nathan that they must collide, they stopped dead in the form of a cross and slowly began to revolve. At their centre a new light grew—one which was large and brilliantly white—and once formed it winked like a heliograph, repeating the same sequence of flashes five or six times over. Then, gradually, the whole thing faded.

'What was *that*?' asked Nathan.

Mr Gentleman only smiled, however, and continued staring up at the stars.

Other books by Stephen Elboz

The House of Rats
ISBN 0 19 275021 6

Winner of the 1992 Smarties Young Judges Prize for the 9–11 age category

One damp foggy morning, the man who called himself the master threw down his napkin and strode out from the great house, never to return.

Esther, Zachary, Carl and Frankie are happy, living in the mysterious great house, until suddenly the master vanishes and everything changes. The safe routines disappear. The wolves which roam the forest outside, howling for food, become a real threat; while inside the house, other people start to take over their lives.

Without realizing it, the children are in great danger. But then, just when they think there can be no escape, they meet one of the 'Rats'. And they begin to discover the secrets of the amazing house.

'I loved the vividly realised characters, the warmth and wit of *The House of Rats*. This is a fine novel.'
Times Educational Supplement

'A brilliant story which grips you from the first to last page.'
Mail on Sunday

Temmi and the Flying Bears
ISBN 0 19 275015 1

The men arrived at Temmi's village one snowy winter's evening . . .

'We have been sent by command of the great Witch herself. She has heard of a rarity found only in these parts. A species of bear with wings. And it is her noble majesty's wish to present one of these freakish creatures to her daughter, Princess Agna.'

Temmi tries to stop the soldiers, but it is no use. The little flying bear cub, Cush, is captured and injured, and Temmi knows he has no choice but to look after Cush, even if it means becoming a prisoner in the Witch-Queen's castle. But the Witch is dying, and when the Young Princess Agna becomes Queen, Temmi finds that it's not just Cush and himself he now has to save.

Will Temmi and Cush ever get home again? And can they survive after finding out about the secrets of the Ice Castle?

'A beautifully written fantasy which will hold the reader's attention from page one . . . a story of good and evil, warmth and cold, so brilliantly described by the author that you will shiver as you read.'

The School Librarian